Murder in the Bay

LOTTIE SPRIGG COUNTRY HOUSE MYSTERY BOOK 4

MARTHA BOND

Lottie Sprigg Country House Mystery Series

* * *

Murder in the Library
Murder in the Grotto
Murder in the Maze
Murder in the Bay

Chapter One

'Is EVERYTHING ALRIGHT, LOTTIE?' asked Mrs Moore. They were breakfasting in her Chelsea home.

'I don't know.'

'Who's the letter from?'

Lottie's hands trembled as she held it. 'It's from Josephine Holmes.'

'One of the many Josephines you've written to?'

'Yes.'

'And?'

'She says she's the lady who asked about me at the orphanage.'

Mrs Moore dropped her teacup into its saucer, sloshing her tea.

'Good golly, Lottie. Do you mind if I read it?'

'Not at all.'

Lottie handed her the letter, then fed a piece of smoked kipper to her corgi, Rosie, as Mrs Moore read it.

'"Dear Miss Sprigg",' said Mrs Moore. '"Thank you for your letter, I apologise for my late reply. I had to build up my courage before I wrote this. I am the lady who was asking after

1

you in the orphanage. Please do reply to me once you receive this. Yours sincerely, Miss Josephine Holmes." Well I never, Lottie. Do you think this letter has come from your mother?'

'I'd like to think so. Why else would she have asked after me at the orphanage?'

'Well, there's only one way of finding out.' She passed the letter back to Lottie. 'You'll have to reply to her.'

Lottie's mind emptied as she struggled to comprehend the news in the letter. 'But what do I say?'

Mrs Moore laughed. 'It's astonishing how moments like this can suddenly make us tongue-tied, isn't it? You could thank her for replying to you. Maybe you could tell her about your search for your mother. Then perhaps you can tell her a bit about yourself. A little story about your life.'

'Would she be interested?'

'If she's your mother, Lottie, then she'll be extremely interested! She'll want to know everything about you.'

'Alright then.' Lottie felt her shoulders sink beneath an unseen weight.

'You look pensive,' said Mrs Moore. 'What's the matter?'

'I'm not sure. Perhaps I'm worried she won't want to know about me. I'm worried she won't be interested in me.'

'She replied to your letter, didn't she?'

'But she says it took her a while to reply.'

'Because it means a lot to her, Lottie. Just as it means a lot to you. These things aren't easy. But if you can write her a nice chatty letter, then hopefully she'll do the same. With time, the pair of you could arrange to meet.'

'Goodness.' Lottie's stomach fluttered. 'It all seems too much.'

'That's because it is.' Mrs Moore reached across the table and squeezed her hand. 'I think it's wonderful news, Lottie. But you can take your time with this. Reply to Miss Holmes when you feel ready to do so. In the meantime, we've got a lovely trip to Fernwood-on-Sea in the west country to look forward to.'

'Fernwood-on-Sea?'

'Yes, I've received a letter this morning from my dear old friend, Lady Florence Cavendish. She went through a divorce a few years ago. Her former husband went off to America after the divorce but has put in a surprise reappearance. She says in her letter that it's all been a bit difficult and she would appreciate some company. I don't know about you, Lottie, but with the glorious weather that's forecast for the next week or so, I fancy a trip to the seaside. How about you?'

Chapter Two

LOTTIE, Rosie and Mrs Moore travelled by train to the west country. The journey slowed a little as the train navigated the rolling hills of the Devon countryside before running alongside the rocky coastline.

'Isn't it lovely to see the sea again, Lottie?' said Mrs Moore. 'We haven't seen it since our return from the continent. Hopefully, it will be warm enough for a dip. Lady Florence's house overlooks a beautiful bay. And she has her own beach! I really can't wait to visit the place again.'

They disembarked at a countryside railway station. White picket fencing lined the edge of the platform, and the rustic station building was adorned with pots of vibrant summer flowers.

A sombre-faced man in a blue uniform greeted them and introduced himself as Langley. He and the station porter loaded their trunks into a long, shiny car. The drive to Lady Florence's home took them along winding country lanes where tall hedgerows were speckled with wildflowers.

They passed over the brow of a hill to see a strip of blue,

4

twinkling sea. And just before it, nestled among trees, a large house gleamed in the sunshine.

Mrs Moore pulled out her lorgnette and admired the view through the car window. 'Tidecrest House,' she announced. 'That's where we shall be staying, Lottie!'

They got a close-up view of the house once they had travelled along a meandering, tree-lined driveway. It was built of cream stone and had rows of tall windows and a large columned porch. A wisteria clambered up the walls and over the porch with hanging blooms of frothy lilac flowers.

Two ladies stepped out of the house as Langley stopped the car in front of the door.

'Here's Lady Florence and her companion, Miss Trent,' said Mrs Moore. 'Lady Florence is the one in blue.'

Lottie would have had little trouble guessing which was which. Lady Florence had a haughty expression and bobbed silver hair. She wore an elegant sapphire dress with a low waist and billowy sheer sleeves. Miss Trent was apple-cheeked with wavy brown hair. She wore a tweed skirt, white blouse and beige cardigan.

'Roberta!' cried out Lady Florence as Langley opened the car door. 'It's been too long!'

'It has indeed,' said Mrs Moore as she climbed out of the car and greeted her old friend.

Lottie and Rosie followed Mrs Moore and were greeted by a friendly black labrador with a grey muzzle.

After the introductions, Lady Florence told them to follow her into the house. 'We're having tea on the terrace,' said Lady Florence. 'And after that, I shall show you around. Come along, Duke!'

At this command, the labrador trotted at her heel.

They walked through the large entrance hall, passed a sweeping staircase, and entered a drawing room with tall doors standing open onto a terrace. Long silk curtains moved gently in the breeze.

'I'd forgotten how beautiful it is here,' said Mrs Moore as they stepped out onto the terrace. The lawn slipped down to a small, wooded area by the bay. Lottie could hear the waves washing up onto the beach.

To their left, a rocky headland jutted out into the sea, Lottie could make out the silhouette of a church on the clifftop. To their right, Lottie could see Fernwood-on-Sea: a cluster of rooftops and white and pink walls. Its walled harbour was filled with boats. Beyond the village rose another headland. Its green slopes were dotted with tiny white specks of sheep.

'I never tire of this view,' said Lady Florence.

'I'm not surprised,' said Mrs Moore. 'You must be the envy of all the locals.'

Lady Florence gave a laugh. 'You're not wrong, Roberta.'

Chapter Three

LADY FLORENCE GESTURED for them to sit at the table on the terrace. It was covered with a gingham tablecloth and laid out for afternoon tea. There were china teapots, jugs of lemonade and platters of delicate sandwiches and colourful bite-sized cakes. Lottie's mouth watered.

'How wonderful, Florence,' said Mrs Moore. 'I really don't know where to start!'

'No need to make a fuss,' said Lady Florence. 'Just tuck in.'

Rosie and Duke trotted around the terrace together, then Miss Trent found a ball for them and threw it onto the lawn. Duke grabbed the ball and Rosie tried to steal it. A good-natured game ensued.

'I think I remember saying this before,' said Mrs Moore. 'But that clifftop is a funny place for a church.'

'It was much needed in its day,' said Lady Florence. 'The churchyard is filled with sailors who lost their lives in wrecks on the rocks there. It's called Ashford Point, but it's always been known locally as Shipwreck Point.'

Mrs Moore gave a shiver. 'Goodness. What a name.'

Lottie felt a thrill of excitement. She liked the idea of exploring Shipwreck Point.

'I'm actually descended from a shipwrecked sailor,' said Miss Trent with a smile. 'My great grandfather was Dutch and was rescued from the bay when his ship hit the rocks. He was so impressed by the friendliness of everyone in Fernwood-on-Sea that he decided to stay here.'

'That's a lovely story,' said Mrs Moore.

'It is,' said Lady Florence. 'And those were the days when the inhabitants of Fernwood-on-Sea were friendly.'

'Oh dear, are they not friendly anymore?'

'No.'

'Some are,' said Miss Trent.

'No, Marianne. They're not. I've had to put up with Rupert returning from America and making unreasonable demands. Has anyone called on me to offer their sympathy? No, they have not.'

'Oh dear, what's Rupert been doing?' said Mrs Moore.

'He wants to live in this house again.'

'But wasn't it decided during your divorce that the house is yours?'

'Yes. He's being a nuisance.'

'Have you seen much of him since he returned to England?'

'Unfortunately, I have. He's taken rooms at the Star Hotel in Fernwood-on-Sea.'

'Can't you ban him from entering the house?'

'I might have to do that if he continues to annoy me. I just wish he'd go away again.'

'Why did he come back?'

'He hasn't given me a detailed explanation, but I suspect his business didn't do as well as he had hoped.'

'What was his business?'

'Something to do with the chemical industry, apparently. He has no expertise in that area, all he had was money to invest in it. So I suspect the money's gone, and he's come crawling back.' She took a sip of tea. 'I'm rather embarrassed to say this, but he has suggested a reconciliation. After our twenty-five-year marriage ended in divorce! Can you believe it? I don't imagine for one moment that he's still in love with me. I think he only suggested it because he wants to live in the house.'

'Dear oh dear, Florence. I am sorry to hear it,' said Mrs Moore. 'After going through the pain of a divorce, it's not right that you should be faced with your former spouse like this again.'

'It's not right. And the only person who's shown any sympathy for me is Marianne.'

Miss Trent gave a sad nod.

'Well, hopefully Lottie and I can cheer you up for the next few days, Florence!' said Mrs Moore. 'And if you want me to have a word with Rupert and tell him to stay away, then I'll be more than happy to do so.'

'Thank you, Roberta.' She removed her serviette from her lap and placed it on the table. 'Now, shall I show you around? A few things have probably changed since you last visited.'

Having worked as a maid for Mrs Moore's sister at Fortescue Manor, Lottie was accustomed to grand country houses. But she was still impressed by Tidecrest House and its beautiful furnishings.

Lady Florence led them through a series of rooms, pointing out fine paintings, ornaments and pieces of furniture. 'I suppose I'm quite lucky that all this is mine now,' she said. 'Rupert took a lot of the money, but I suspect he's frittered most of it away. As for me, I still have all this. It's wonderful, isn't it?'

'It certainly is,' said Mrs Moore. 'And you own the beach too, don't you?'

'Oh yes. I have a hundred acres here, and that includes the beach. Shall we take a little walk down there now? It will give the maids a little more time to unpack your things, and then you can go and freshen up in your rooms when we get back.'

Chapter Four

THE DOGS FOLLOWED them as they walked across the sloping lawns to a little path which led into woodland. The path wound a short distance through scented ornamental shrubs and trees before leading them out onto the beach.

Lottie's feet sank into the soft golden sand and Rosie paused for a moment, examining the new surface beneath her paws. Then she cantered off after Duke, who was already paddling in the waves.

'This is such a beautiful spot, Florence,' said Mrs Moore. 'And your boathouse has been repainted since I was last here.' She gestured at the wooden building at the end of the beach. 'Do you still sail?'

'Oh yes, most days,' said Lady Florence. 'The boathouse has been redone. Come and have a look at it.'

Lottie, Mrs Moore and Miss Trent followed her along a weathered timber walkway which had been laid across the sand.

'Have you got a key on you, Marianne?'

'Yes, my lady.'

Miss Trent opened the door and the hinges gave a loud squeak.

Lady Florence winced. 'I've told Arthur to oil this door and he hasn't done it yet.'

There was a small sailing boat inside the boathouse and a pleasant smell of wood and seawater. Lottie could hear the waves beyond the large double doors at the far end. Ropes looped down from the timber rafters and pots of paints and oils sat on a workbench. A row of heavy tools hung above the workbench, next to a large map of the bay. A window on the opposite side offered a view of the beach, and it had a couple of comfy chairs beneath it. A pile of sailing magazines sat on a little table next to one of the chairs.

'Didn't you have a bigger boat the last time I visited, Florence?' asked Mrs Moore.

'Yes. That's when Rupert and I used to go sailing together. But I have this little one now, it's only twelve feet. A size I can manage on my own.'

'You manage that on your own?' said Mrs Moore. 'I'm not sure I could.'

'That's because you haven't been sailing for thirty years like I have.'

'I suppose so.' Mrs Moore turned to Miss Trent. 'Am I right in remembering you don't sail, Marianne?'

'I don't.' Miss Trent shook her head. 'Even though my great grandfather was a sailor! I don't like all that bobbing up and down on the sea.'

'I can't say I enjoy it enormously either,' said Mrs Moore. 'I fell from a gondola into a Venice canal once.' Lady Florence laughed. 'I don't mind a boat ride,' continued Mrs Moore, 'but I much prefer dry land.'

Lady Florence gave a laugh. 'Landlubbers! Come on, let's find the dogs.'

They left the boathouse and returned to the beach.

Duke was swimming in the sea while Rosie paddled in the shallows. Each time a wave receded, she splashed out to sea. But when a wave came in, she darted back to the shore.

'How funny!' said Mrs Moore. 'I'm not sure Rosie knows what to do with the sea yet. Will you be going sailing today, Florence?'

'No, not today. There's no wind at all. Look at the sea, it's as flat as a millpond.'

'My ideal boating conditions,' said Mrs Moore with a chuckle.

'The forecast says some wind will pick up late tomorrow afternoon,' said Miss Trent.

'That's right, Marianne. That'll be my next opportunity.'

A barking dog interrupted them. Lottie turned to see a terrier running across the beach from the harbour wall at the far end. In the distance was a loping figure of a man.

'Oh dear,' said Lady Florence. 'He shouldn't be here!'

'I thought your beach was private, Lady Florence?' said Mrs Moore.

'Yes, it is. But try telling the locals that! I've got signs up saying "private property", but I don't want to put up ugly fences all over the place.'

Rosie disliked the barking terrier and ran to Lottie's side for reassurance. The terrier stood on the shoreline, growling at Duke, who remained in the sea.

The man was closer to them now. He was wearing hiking trousers, a shirt and a boater hat.

'Good afternoon!' He raised his hat in greeting.

Lady Florence tutted.

He was a handsome, grey-haired man in his fifties. 'Lovely day!' he said.

Lady Florence sighed.

'Who is this gentleman?' Mrs Moore asked.

'Dr Edward Blackwood.'

13

'Come here, Brutus!' the doctor said to his dog. The terrier ignored him.

He joined the group of women and gave them a broad smile. An uncomfortable silence followed, and Lottie couldn't fathom why.

'I'm Dr Blackwood.' He held out his hand to Mrs Moore, and she shook it.

'Mrs Moore. An old friend of Lady Florence's. And this is my assistant, Miss Sprigg.'

'Lovely to meet you!'

Lottie smiled in reply. Rosie sniffed the doctor's legs.

Lady Florence remained silent, and Lottie noticed Miss Trent's face had flushed red.

'Are you staying for long?' Dr Blackwood asked Mrs Moore.

'No, only a few days. We thought we'd treat ourselves to some time by the sea. It really is quite beautiful down here.'

'It is indeed.' He fixed Lady Florence's gaze, and another uncomfortable pause followed.

'Do I have to remind you again that this is my beach, Dr Blackwood?' said Lady Florence. 'It's private property.'

'No, you don't need to remind me, Florence.'

'Lady Florence to you.'

'Lady Florence. I'm afraid I'm being a naughty boy again.' He slapped his own wrist, then grinned. 'But the detour is such an awfully long walk. I'm walking from the harbour there.' He looked over his shoulder and pointed back at the harbour wall. 'And I want to join the public path which leads up to Shipwreck Point.' He turned back and pointed to the rocky headland beyond the boathouse. 'This beach really is the easiest way to access it.'

'Pure laziness, Dr Blackwood,' said Lady Florence. 'There is no harm in following the road for a mile instead. And besides, it's splendid exercise.'

'Yes, it's good exercise alright. I was taking a chance today and hoping I wouldn't see you around, Lady Florence.'

'But you did. And if I catch you trespassing on my beach again, I shall have to take formal action.'

'I can assure you it won't happen again. Not until next week, anyway!'

Lady Florence gave him a sharp stare. 'I sincerely hope you're joking, Dr Blackwood.'

'Of course.' He grinned. 'What lovely weather it is today. No good for sailing though.'

'No good at all,' said Lady Florence. 'But it will be breezier tomorrow. Hopefully, I'll get out then. Can you remove yourself and your dog from my beach please?'

'Oh yes!' He grinned again and went to fetch his terrier, who was still barking at Duke.

'Dr Blackwood is insufferable,' said Lady Florence once the doctor had taken the path towards Shipwreck Point.

'Have you fallen out over something?' asked Mrs Moore.

'I don't want to say any more. I refuse to let him ruin my day. How about we walk back up to the house?'

Chapter Five

LADY FLORENCE PAUSED JUST before they took the path back to the house. 'See that promontory over there, Roberta?' She pointed to the headland beyond the village. 'It's known as Windy Edge. Let's walk up there tomorrow for a picnic. It has a delightful view.'

'How long is the walk?' asked Mrs Moore.

'Not long. We walk along the beach, past the harbour in Fernwood-on-Sea, and then we take the path up the hill.'

'It looks quite far away.'

'It's not that far at all. Sometimes the sea haze makes things look more distant.'

'Very well. I like a leisurely stroll, but hiking up a headland on a hot day sounds a bit exhausting.'

'You'll be fine, Roberta. It will do you good. Marianne will carry the picnic for us, won't you, Marianne?'

Miss Trent nodded.

'And if it helps, I'll ask Langley to drive up and collect us in the car. Does that sound fair?'

'I suppose it does,' said Mrs Moore.

'Wonderful! Oh look, here's Arthur.'

16

A stooped, broad man in overalls had arrived on the beach. His face was as weathered and worn as his old brown overalls. He took off his cap and gave the ladies a reverent nod with his bald head. 'Afternoon.'

'You remember Arthur, don't you, Mrs Moore?' said Lady Florence.

'Yes, I do. Hello, Arthur.'

'Afternoon. Fine weather, isn't it?'

'Not for sailing,' said Lady Florence.

'They say the wind will pick up tomorrow.'

'So I've heard. I shall go then.'

'It's nice to see you again, Arthur,' said Mrs Moore. 'You must have worked on this estate for years now.'

'That's right, Mrs Moore. Over fifty years, man and boy. I first worked here for old Mrs Harmsworth. And then Lord and Lady Cavendish when they bought the house.'

'Arthur knows the house and grounds inside out, don't you, Arthur?' said Lady Florence. 'Every square inch. If you ever need help with anything, Mrs Moore, all you need to do is ask Arthur.'

'How wonderful to have a useful chap on hand,' said Mrs Moore.

'You could have done with being here five minutes ago, Arthur,' said Lady Florence. 'I caught Dr Blackwood using my beach as a shortcut again.'

'Is that right, my lady? I've had to tell him a few times now to go by the road.'

'It's ridiculous. I might be forced to put up barbed wire at either end of the beach. Or maybe we need you on patrol with your shotgun, Arthur.'

'I don't think there's any need for that, my lady.'

'There will be if we don't solve the trespassing problem. I'd like you to keep a closer eye on this beach please, Arthur. Make sure nobody walks across it.'

'Yes, my lady. I've come down to oil the hinges on the boathouse door.'

'About time too. I can't abide the dreadful squeak they make.'

'It's the salty air,' he said. 'Makes everything rust faster.'

'I can only hope that doesn't happen to me!' said Lady Florence, laughing loudly at her joke.

'No chance of that, my lady,' said Arthur as he sauntered on.

Chapter Six

THEY SET off for their picnic on Windy Edge the following morning. Lady Florence led the way with Duke at her side. She wore stylish sports trousers with a blouse, sunhat and sturdy walking shoes. Mrs Moore didn't own a pair of trousers, so she wore a long summer dress and carried a parasol. Lottie wore a sunhat and a plain cotton dress which was perfect for summer days. Miss Trent brought up the rear. She was dressed in brown tweed and had the enormous picnic hamper strapped to her back.

'Would you like a hand carrying something?' Lottie asked her.

'Oh no, I'm fine. Quite used to it. Thank you, Miss Sprigg.'

Rosie enjoyed being on the beach again. She skipped in the breaking waves, then sniffed the air as they approached the harbour. Some steps took them up and over the harbour wall, and they arrived in the village of Fernwood-on-Sea.

An old stone seawall enclosed the harbour. The scent of drying seaweed and fish filled the air and seagulls cruised lazily overhead. A row of crooked little shops and houses overlooked the harbour. They huddled together, as if protecting themselves from the coastal winds.

'There's a little more breeze today,' said Lady Florence. 'I'm looking forward to it picking up later.'

'Someone's waving at us,' said Mrs Moore.

'Oh dear, who?'

'The man on that boat. He's got a large beard.'

Lady Florence tutted. 'Captain O'Malley.'

He wore a fisherman's smock and stood at the bow of an old blue fishing trawler. It had a tall mast and a small dirty white cabin. Lottie could see the name on the weatherworn plaque on the bow: The Golden Herring.

'Ahoy there!' he called out.

'Oh, good grief.' Lady Florence gave him a quick wave and kept walking.

'You don't want to speak to Captain O'Malley?' asked Mrs Moore.

'Not particularly.'

They continued on their way and the headland of Windy Edge loomed ominously ahead of them. Lottie noticed Mrs Moore glance longingly at a little tea shop with a striped awning and tables set outside. Next to it sat a seafood restaurant with fresh white paintwork and a board displaying a tasty menu.

They left the village, climbed over a stile into a field, and began walking up the hillside. A group of horses watched them, flicking their tails at the flies.

Mrs Moore paused while Lady Florence and Miss Trent marched on ahead. 'I've stopped to admire the view, Lottie,' she puffed.

Birdsong and the bleating of sheep carried on the breeze. They looked out at the view across the bay while Rosie sat down in the shade of a hedgerow. The sea dazzled in the sunlight and Tidecrest House gleamed on its hill above the village and beach.

'It really is a beautiful place to live, isn't it?' said Mrs Moore, surveying the scene through her lorgnette. 'No wonder everyone is so envious of Florence in her lovely home.'

'Come along!' came a shout from further up the hill.

Mrs Moore groaned. 'Florence is a good friend of mine,' she whispered to Lottie. 'But sometimes she can be terribly bossy.'

They continued their climb up the hill.

'Thank goodness Langley is picking us up after this,' panted Mrs Moore. 'Although he could have brought us here, too. On a cooler day, I wouldn't mind. But it's so warm!'

Eventually, the ground flattened out and the hedgerows made way for an expanse of grass on the clifftop. To their left was a precipitous drop to the sea.

Lady Florence, Duke and Miss Trent stood waiting for them.

'You finally made it,' said Lady Florence. 'Although I can't say it's been worth your while.'

'No?' Mrs Moore could barely find the breath to say anything else.

'No.' Lady Florence shot a glance at a large group of people gathered nearby. 'I'm afraid our picnic is going to be completely ruined.'

Chapter Seven

'RUINED?' panted Mrs Moore. She was still trying to recover from the climb up the headland.

'Yes. The Fitzroy family is here.'

'Isn't there enough space for all of us?' asked Mrs Moore. Lottie surveyed the vast green expanse of Windy Edge. The family group sat about a hundred yards away. Some had chairs, while others sat on the ground. Children played around them and two large motor cars were parked a short distance from them. Lottie could see a trestle table laden with food. The ladies were dressed in pale colours and wore large summer hats. The men wore light-coloured suits. The sound of laughter drifted over to them. Lottie wondered why Lady Florence found the Fitzroys so objectionable.

'We can sit over there,' said Mrs Moore, pointing to a patch of grass some distance away. 'We won't have to have anything to do with them.'

'I've managed to go six weeks without seeing a single member of the Fitzroy family,' said Lady Florence. 'But the moment I decide to come up to Windy Edge for a picnic, I discover they've had the same idea! It's a disgrace.'

'I'm sure you can pretend they're not here, Florence,' said Mrs Moore.

'How can I pretend that? I can hear their laughter. I can see them whenever I glance in that direction.'

'Then don't glance in their direction,' said Mrs Moore. 'They're not spoiling the view, are they? I think if we lay our blanket down over there, we can look at the sea and enjoy the beautiful view with no disturbance from them.'

'Mrs Moore is right, Lady Florence,' said Miss Trent. 'We can sit with our backs to them and have a wonderful time.'

'Very well,' said Lady Florence stiffly.

Lottie helped Miss Trent lay out the picnic blankets and unpack the food.

'I see the Fitzroys have brought a table and chairs with them,' said Lady Florence.

'That's because they've travelled here by car,' said Mrs Moore. 'But we did it the proper way. We walked, Florence. Now don't give them another thought.'

They settled down on the blankets. The centrepiece of the picnic was a large chicken pie. Lottie had to keep a close eye on Rosie to make sure she didn't sample it. There was an array of sandwiches, stuffed eggs, potato salad, cuts of cold meat, little leaves of lettuce, and tomatoes. Lottie was also delighted to spot strawberries and scones with little pots of jam and cream. Miss Trent produced a little stove, a small kettle, teapot and cups.

'Golly,' said Mrs Moore. 'I can't quite believe you carried all this here, Marianne.'

Miss Trent smiled. 'Tea, Mrs Moore?'

'Yes please.'

They tucked into the food.

'Simply wonderful,' said Mrs Moore. 'I've travelled to many places in my time, but there's nothing quite like a picnic by the sea on a perfect English summer's day, is there?'

No sooner had she spoken, when a football landed with a splat in the middle of the chicken pie.

Chapter Eight

'Oh, good grief!' Lady Florence leapt to her feet. 'Our lovely picnic! Ruined!'

Lottie turned to see a freckle-faced boy cautiously approaching. He was about seven and wore short trousers and a grass-stained shirt. 'I'm terribly sorry,' he stammered. 'Please may I have my ball back?'

Lady Florence bent down and snatched up the ball. 'No!'

The boy's face crumpled. Then he turned and ran to the Fitzroy family group.

'Goodness, Florence,' said Mrs Moore. 'Although it's dreadfully annoying that the chicken pie is ruined, everything else is absolutely fine. It was only an accident.'

'He shouldn't have kicked it in our direction,' said Lady Florence. 'And it's extremely foolish to allow young children to play with a ball on a clifftop. So typical of the Fitzroy family. They have absolutely no idea about anything.'

She pulled a hatpin from her sun hat.

'Oh Florence,' said Mrs Moore. 'Surely not?'

'They asked for it!' The long, sharp hatpin glimmered in the sunlight.

'But he's just a boy.'

'Who should know better!' Lady Florence raised her hand, then jabbed the hatpin into the football.

Lottie watched in horror as the ball slowly deflated. It took about a minute. And during that time, there was no sound other than the hiss of escaping air. Lady Florence sat down, then finished the job by squeezing the ball in her lap to expel the last bit of air. She then tossed the floppy leather carcass onto the grass nearby.

Lottie and Mrs Moore exchanged a wide-eyed glance.

Then they caught sight of a dark-haired lady in a lilac summer dress walking towards them. 'Good afternoon!' she called out as she approached.

'Victoria Fitzroy,' muttered Lady Florence as she pushed her hatpin back into place. 'Dreadful woman.'

'Hello, Lady Florence. I'm so sorry to be troubling you when you're enjoying a picnic with your friends. But my son's ball accidentally landed close by and I wondered if I could retrieve it for him.'

Lady Florence got to her feet. 'It didn't land close by, Mrs Fitzroy. It landed in our chicken pie!'

'I do apologise. I've had a strong word with my son about it. And I shall make sure that we have a replacement pie sent to you from the bakery in the village at the earliest opportunity.'

'That doesn't help us now though, does it?'

'No, it doesn't. And I can only apologise again for my son's behaviour. He got rather carried away with himself.'

'You shouldn't let your child kick a ball about on a cliff top,' said Lady Florence. 'It's a silly place to play ball and also rather dangerous.'

'While I appreciate the advice, Lady Florence, my son knows not to stray anywhere near the edge of the cliff. As punishment for ruining your picnic, I shall put his ball in the car so he won't be able to kick it anymore while we're up here.'

'Very well.' Lady Florence stooped down, picked up the flabby ball and tossed it to her. Mrs Fitzroy gasped as she caught it.

'I'm afraid that's what he gets for kicking his ball into our pie,' said Lady Florence.

Mrs Fitzroy clenched her jaw, then scowled. 'There really was no need for this! I'm not sure you noticed, Lady Florence, but I was polite and courteous to you just then. I apologised for my son's mistake, and I offered to make amends. And this is your response?' She held up the saggy sack. 'What a cruel woman you are. As each year passes by, I hope in vain that you'll become a nicer person. But every single encounter I have with you is miserable. Your pride and grudges get in the way of every possible relationship. You have no interest in getting on with people, and you're only interested in raising yourself above them. I'd like to think better of you, but you're petty, pedantic, and very, very rude.' She turned and marched back to the family group.

An awkward silence fell, and Lady Florence sat down on the blanket again.

'I apologise for that, Mrs Moore and Miss Sprigg,' she said. 'You have now encountered the Fitzroy family. I'm sure you can understand now why I dislike them so much.'

'Indeed,' said Mrs Moore. 'But Victoria Fitzroy was polite and apologetic when she first approached you.'

'Oh yes, she prides herself on being better than everyone else. But the fact is she's a terrible mother who doesn't know how to control her child. And she's a member of the Fitzroy family, which is a crime in itself.' She looked at her watch. 'I suggest we pack up our things now. Langley will be here soon.'

Chapter Nine

'LORD CAVENDISH IS HERE, MY LADY,' said the po-faced butler when they returned to Tidecrest House.

'Oh no! Today really is turning out to be quite troublesome indeed. What does he want?'

'He didn't say, my lady. I told him you were out, and he said he would wait.' He gave Mrs Moore and Lottie a sidelong glance. 'I also informed him that you had guests, but he told me that the matter would be quick.'

'Very well, then. Where is he?'

'He's out on the terrace, my lady.'

'Right then.' Lady Florence linked her arm through Mrs Moore's. 'You can come with me.'

'Oh no, I don't think that would be right,' said Mrs Moore. 'Clearly this is something which you and Rupert need to sort out between you.'

'I don't wish to have a long, detailed conversation with him. If you're with me, he'll have to keep it brief. Let's all four of us go out onto the terrace. He won't like it one bit and will hopefully scarper.'

Out on the terrace, a breeze was picking up and a few clouds were appearing in the sky.

Lord Cavendish lounged in a chair with a pipe in his mouth. He was a stocky, red-faced man with a large, grey handlebar moustache. He got to his feet when he saw them and smoothed his pale linen suit.

'Mrs Moore!' He took his pipe from his mouth and fixed a smile. 'It's been some years since I last saw you. How the devil are you?'

'I'm quite well, thank you, Rupert. I hear you've been living in America.'

'Yes, I have. I had an interesting few years out there. I went into business with an old school friend of mine. It didn't go as smoothly as I expected, so now I find myself back on these shores.'

'I'm sorry to hear it, Rupert. It's lovely to see you again. This is my assistant, Miss Sprigg.'

He gave Lottie a polite nod. 'Good afternoon, miss. And is this your dog?'

'Yes. She's called Rosie.'

'I love corgis.' He bent down and patted Rosie's head. 'The wind's picking up,' he said.

'Yes, I shall go sailing later,' said Lady Florence. 'Now, as you can see, Rupert, I have guests. What do you wish to talk to me about?'

'I'm sorry to intrude, Florence, but I wish to have a few words with you in private.'

'That won't be possible.'

'Oh.'

'I'm entertaining my guests, Rupert.'

'I see. But it won't take more than a few minutes.'

'Whatever you have to say, you can say it in front of Marianne and my guests.'

'I'd rather not.'

'Well, you've wasted your time coming here today then, haven't you?'

Lord Cavendish returned his pipe to his mouth and sucked on it thoughtfully before removing it again. 'Very well. I came here today to find out if you've made your mind up.'

'Made my mind up about what?'

'That matter we discussed last week. I don't particularly want to spell it out, Florence, we have company. I think you know what I'm referring to. So I've come to find out your answer.'

'My answer is no, Rupert.'

His face fell. 'No?'

'I'm afraid so.'

'But you told me you'd think about it.'

'And I have done. And I have reached the conclusion that my answer is no.'

'No to everything?'

'Yes, absolutely. No to everything. You can't just take yourself off to America whenever you wish, Rupert, and then come back here with your tail between your legs hoping I'll forgive and forget everything. It really isn't that simple.'

'Right.' He gave a sigh. 'It sounds like your mind is quite made up on the matter, Florence. But are you really sure?'

'I've never been so sure in all my life.'

'I see. Well, that really is quite disappointing, Florence. Very disappointing indeed.'

He put his pipe back in his mouth and surveyed the grounds, as if regretting everything around him was no longer his.

'I shall leave you to it, then,' he said eventually.

'Goodbye Rupert.'

Lord Cavendish went on his way.

'Golly, Florence,' said Mrs Moore, once he'd left. 'Was Rupert's question regarding the reconciliation?'

'Yes,' said Lady Florence. 'Ridiculous isn't it? I don't know how he could possibly think I want to be with him again. We're divorced! And it's only because he's lost all his money and wants this house. The sooner he realises he has no chance, the better. Now let's go and have tea. I shan't be dining with you tonight because I'm going sailing. But you'll keep Marianne company, won't you?'

'Of course,' said Mrs Moore.

Chapter Ten

LOTTIE BEGAN a letter to Josephine Holmes before dinner that evening. She sat on her bed with Rosie by her side and chewed the end of her pen.

Dear Miss Holmes, she wrote. *Thank you very much for your letter.*

She turned to her dog. 'I don't know what to write next, Rosie.'

The bell rang for dinner.

Lottie, Mrs Moore and Miss Trent sat down to an evening meal of onion soup followed by lemon sole with a tasty parsley sauce.

Lady Florence popped in to see them. 'I'm off now.' She wore a short-sleeved blouse, slacks, and deck shoes. 'Don't wait up. I'll watch the sunset from the water and will be back late.'

'Have a lovely time, Florence,' said Mrs Moore. 'We'll look out for you bobbing about on the sea.'

'You do that. Cheerio.'

They returned to their food.

'Florence has remarkable energy for a lady of her age,' said Mrs Moore. 'I daren't ask her how old she is, but I think she could be a few years older than me.'

'She puts it down to never having had children,' said Miss Trent. 'She says children tire you out.'

'I've never had children, either. So why am I so tired out?'

Miss Trent gave a little laugh. 'I'm afraid I don't know the answer to that, Mrs Moore.'

'I take it Lady Florence's dislike of children is the reason she punctured that young boy's ball on Windy Edge today.'

'I don't think she dislikes children. The reason she punctured the ball was because he's a Fitzroy.'

'Why does she dislike the family so much?'

'Lots of reasons. And the feeling is mutual. Lord and Lady Fitzroy are envious of Tidecrest House. They live at Fairhaven Manor about half-a-mile inland. It has nice grounds, but it's not by the sea and isn't nearly as beautiful as this place. Lady Florence looks down on the Fitzroys because Lord Fitzroy's grandfather made his money in coal mining. His title wasn't hereditary, it was bestowed upon him by the government of the day. Lord Cavendish's family title goes back to medieval days, so that makes his family more important.'

'I see. And the lady we encountered on Windy Edge?'

'That's Victoria Fitzroy. She married Lord and Lady Fitzroy's son, Jasper. He was killed in the war.'

'Oh dear. That poor little boy has lost his father.'

'Yes, it's sad. But Victoria Fitzroy is a nuisance.'

'Why's that?'

'She's been using the Fitzroy family's money to buy property. If she continues, she'll own half of Fernwood-on-Sea before long. And when she buys properties, she's put the rent up for the tenants.'

'Oh dear.'

'In fact, my mother's cottage was at risk. The landlord put it up for sale, and Victoria Fitzroy was about to buy it, but Lady Florence outbid her and bought it instead. She couldn't bear the thought of my mother having to pay rent to Victoria Fitzroy. I'm very grateful to Lady Florence for what she did. But Victoria Fitzroy didn't like it one bit.'

'Is there anyone in the village who Lady Florence is on good terms with?'

Miss Trent considered this as she chewed her food. 'No,' she said eventually. 'I don't think there is. Oh goodness, is that the time?'

The clock on the mantelpiece showed it was seven o'clock.

'Do you have to be somewhere, Marianne?' asked Mrs Moore.

'Erm, yes.' She wiped her mouth with her serviette. 'I have to make a telephone call.'

Chapter Eleven

THE FOLLOWING day dawned bright and sunny again. Lottie woke early and got up to take Rosie for a walk in the gardens before breakfast.

At the foot of the stairs, she encountered Miss Trent.

'Oh hello, Miss Sprigg.' She looked pale and was biting her lip.

'Good morning,' said Lottie. 'Is something wrong?'

'Yes. I'm rather worried about Lady Florence. She didn't return last night.'

'She didn't come back from sailing?'

'I don't think so. I took her tea up to her bedroom this morning, and it was empty! Her bed's not been slept in all night. Arthur's gone down to the beach to see if there's any sign of her. Oh dear, my legs feel weak.' Lottie helped her sit on the bottom stair. 'I can't bear the thought of anything awful happening to her!'

Lottie felt worried too, but she tried her best to keep Miss Trent calm. 'There could be a good explanation for why she didn't return to her room last night. Does she ever sleep in her boathouse?'

'No, never. Perhaps she got caught up in a squall. She shouldn't have gone sailing alone!'

'But she often sailed alone, didn't she?'

'Yes. Oh, I feel all shaky.'

Rosie nuzzled her nose into Miss Trent's hand as if comforting her.

Arthur appeared by the staircase. He held his cap in his hand and his face was pale.

Miss Trent let out a gasp. 'What is it, Arthur? Just tell me. I need to know!'

'The boat is in the boathouse,' he said.

'So she got back?'

'I don't know if she went out in the first place.'

'What do you mean?'

'Lady Florence is in the boathouse too,' he said. 'But...'

'Oh no!' cried out Miss Trent. 'Oh, please don't tell me, Arthur. She's dead, isn't she?'

Chapter Twelve

DETECTIVE LYNTON WORE a neat tweed suit and had a tidy steel-grey moustache. He had arranged the chairs in the drawing room so they were all facing his position in front of the fireplace.

'Now let's get a handle on events, shall we?' he said. 'Who was the last person to see Lady Florence alive?'

Mrs Moore raised her hand. 'Well, I suppose that could be us,' she said. She was ashen-faced with red-rimmed eyes. 'And by us, I mean me, Miss Sprigg and Miss Trent. We were in the dining room when Florence popped in to say goodbye.'

'And what time is this?'

'About half-past six or a quarter-to-seven. I know it was before seven because that was when Miss Trent went off to make a telephone call.'

Detective Lynton wrote this down in his notebook. 'Did anyone here see Lady Florence after she left the dining room yesterday evening?'

Everyone shook their heads.

The detective turned to Mrs Moore. 'Why didn't Lady Florence dine with you?' he asked.

'She wanted to go sailing at that time. Something to do with the wind being the right strength and direction. I'm not a sailor myself, so I don't understand these things.'

'And Miss Trent,' said the detective. 'You went off to make a telephone call at seven o'clock. From where did you make that call?'

'Lady Florence's study.'

'And would you mind telling me the nature of the call?'

'I tried to telephone an elderly aunt, but the operator told me there was no answer from the other end.'

'And what did you do after your failed attempt to telephone your elderly aunt?'

'I realised the study was a little messy, so I did some tidying in there.'

'And Mrs Moore,' said the detective. 'Where did you go after you finished your meal?'

'To the sitting room. Miss Sprigg was with me and her corgi dog, too.'

'And did you stay there for the rest of the evening?'

'Yes. And Miss Trent joined us again after a while.'

'And what time was that, Miss Trent?'

'About eight o'clock, I think.'

'Do you agree with that, Mrs Moore?'

'Yes, I think it was about eight.'

'Very good,' said Detective Lynton. 'So we've yet to find someone who witnessed Lady Florence walking from the house to the boathouse. We know she got there alright because that's where she was found. The doctor estimates she died sometime between seven o'clock and midnight. The cause of death was a blow to the head from a wrench. Mr Arthur Harris says he recognises the wrench as being one which belonged to Lady Florence and had hung with some other tools on the boathouse wall.'

'That's right,' said Arthur.

'Now, what time was it when somebody first became concerned about Lady Florence's whereabouts?'

'It was this morning,' said Miss Trent. 'I took a cup of tea up to her room and she wasn't there!'

'Was no one concerned when she failed to return home last night?'

'She told us she'd be late,' said Miss Trent. 'So Tilly left a door unlocked for her.'

'That's right,' said Tilly, a red-haired maid. 'I lock the doors at eleven o'clock every night when everyone goes to bed. If Lady Florence is still out, then I leave the door to the scullery unlocked, and she comes in that way.'

'Is she often out that late?'

'Not very often, no. But occasionally she was late back, and that's when I would leave the door unlocked.'

'It's quite safe to leave a door unlocked around here, Detective, as I'm sure you're aware,' said the housekeeper. 'I would like to add that some supper was left for Lady Florence in the dining room. However, it was left untouched.'

'So by the time everybody in the household had retired for bed, Lady Florence had not returned,' said Detective Lynton. 'But no one was concerned about this because sometimes Lady Florence would be out until late in the evening.'

'That's right,' said the housekeeper.

'And this morning, Miss Trent raised the alarm at what time?'

'Seven o'clock,' said Miss Trent. 'Lady Florence liked to be woken early. As soon as I saw her room was empty, I knew something had to be wrong. Lady Florence always told me where she was going and what she was doing. It was entirely out of character for her not to return to her room at night. If she ever planned to stay away overnight, then I knew about it in advance.'

'Very well. So a search of the house and grounds was then embarked upon?'

'That's right,' said Miss Trent. 'And when we couldn't find her, Arthur went to the beach.'

'Mr Harris,' said the detective. 'Where did you carry out your search?'

'Well, there were plenty of people in the house searching for Lady Florence, so it made sense to me to have a look around the gardens. But my immediate concern was that she could have met with a sailing accident in the bay. So I went down to the beach to see if there was any sign of her boat.'

'And what did you find?'

'All seemed well in the bay. I found the boathouse unlocked. I knew that if Lady Florence had left the boathouse, she would have locked it.'

'She would have locked it when she went sailing?'

'Yes. She was concerned about people trespassing on the beach. She didn't want anybody going into the boathouse and taking anything.'

'Indeed. So you found the boathouse unlocked. Was Lady Florence's boat in place?'

'Yes, it was. And I don't believe she ever went out in it yesterday evening.'

'What makes you say that?'

'There was no sign of it having been used. The boat was propped up on its rack, the mast was down and everything was dry. She clearly hadn't gone out in the boat. And when I looked down at the floor, there she was.' Arthur covered his face with his hands.

'Very tragic indeed,' said the detective. 'So it seems that Lady Florence never went for her sail in the end. Her assailant attacked her before she could get out onto the water. I think it's likely the attack happened soon after she arrived at the boathouse. Did anyone see anyone suspicious lingering in or near the property yesterday?'

Everyone shook their heads.

'Any visitors?'

'Only Lord Cavendish,' said Miss Trent.

'Lady Florence's former husband?'

'Yes. He's recently returned from America and there have been some disagreements between the pair of them.'

The detective made a note in his notebook. 'What sort of disagreements?'

'Lord Cavendish would like to live in this house again,' said Miss Trent.

He raised an eyebrow. 'Is that so?'

Chapter Thirteen

'WHAT TIME WAS Lord Cavendish here yesterday?' asked Detective Lynton.

'He called in at three o'clock,' said the butler. 'Lady Florence was out at the time, but he insisted on waiting for her. She returned at about half-past three and they had a conversation on the terrace.'

'Which we were party to,' said Mrs Moore. 'In fact, Lady Florence requested that I, Miss Sprigg, and Miss Trent should accompany her. She didn't want to speak to Lord Cavendish alone.'

'And why was that?' asked the detective.

'She hoped our presence would keep the conversation short and Lord Cavendish would soon leave.'

'Was she afraid of him?'

'No, I don't think she was afraid of him,' said Miss Trent. 'But she didn't want a big confrontation with him.'

'And what was the conversation about?'

'Lord Cavendish asked Lady Florence if she had thought about his question and she replied she had,' said Mrs Moore. 'She told him the answer was no.'

'And what was the question?' asked the detective.

'He wanted a reconciliation,' said Miss Trent. 'Lady Florence said it was because he wanted to live in the house again. For some reason, she made him wait a few days for her answer. I suspect she wanted to keep him on tenterhooks. He called in yesterday, intent on receiving an answer from her. And she told him the answer was no.'

'And what was his reaction?'

'He was disappointed,' said Miss Trent. 'But he couldn't rant and rage about it because I was there with Mrs Moore and Miss Sprigg.'

'Is Lord Cavendish prone to ranting and raging?'

'Yes, I've known him to.'

'You know the man well, Miss Trent. Do you think he would have ranted and raged if you, Mrs Moore and Miss Sprigg hadn't been there?'

'Oh yes. He has quite a temper on him.'

'Interesting.' Detective Lynton made some more notes. 'And what time did he leave the house?'

'About ten minutes after we got there,' said Miss Trent. 'I suppose it must have been twenty-to-four or thereabouts.'

'Does anyone know where he went?'

'I imagine he went back to his hotel in the village. He's staying at The Star.'

'And how did he arrive here? By car? On foot?'

'I believe Lord Cavendish walked here from the village,' said the butler. 'And I agree with Miss Trent that he left here at twenty-to-four. I saw him to the door.'

Chapter Fourteen

LATER THAT DAY, Lottie, Rosie, Mrs Moore and Duke walked down to the beach. A constable standing guard by the boathouse acknowledged them with a nod.

Rosie and Duke scampered into the waves. Mrs Moore pulled out her handkerchief and wiped her eyes. 'I still can't believe this has happened, Lottie. Florence was a friend of mine. Not the closest friend, but a friend nonetheless. And now she's gone!'

'It's a dreadful shock,' said Lottie.

'It is indeed. I don't understand how this has happened.' She picked up her lorgnette and surveyed the scene. 'When you look at it, I suppose just about anybody could have gained access to the boathouse. They could have approached the beach from either side of the bay, or they could have walked down from the house. They could even have arrived here by boat.'

'I agree,' said Lottie. 'But the culprit has to be someone who knew Lady Florence was going for a sail.'

'Ah yes. So they either followed her here or laid in wait for her. Now, who knew about her plans?'

'You, me and Miss Trent. And some, if not all, of the household staff.'

'But would anyone outside the household have known?'

'Not unless she mentioned it to them,' said Lottie. 'Or perhaps it was someone who knew Lady Florence well enough that they predicted she would make the most of the wind and go out for a sail.'

'That's a good point, Lottie. Someone who would have known it was a habit of hers to do that. Lord Cavendish perhaps?'

Lottie remembered something. 'Lord Cavendish knew! Don't you remember? When Lady Florence spoke to him on the terrace, he mentioned the wind was picking up.'

'That's right! And he made a comment about Florence going for a sail and she confirmed she would. So he knew about her plans. But how did he know what time she would go? He left here at twenty-to-four. Surely he couldn't have loitered by the boathouse for three hours?'

'Or in it. Maybe he had a key?'

'That's a good point, Lottie. He could have hidden in there, couldn't he? Lord Cavendish seems like the most obvious suspect. Where was he between twenty-to-four and seven o'clock?'

'That's what Detective Lynton will try to find out. There could be other suspects, too. Do you recall Miss Trent telling us that no one in the village was on good terms with Lady Florence?'

'Yes, that was a bit sad to hear. I considered Florence a friend, but I was a little surprised by her hostility towards people during our excursion to Windy Edge. I don't know why she was like that. She tried to ignore that friendly man on the boat in the harbour, didn't she? And deliberately puncturing that little boy's football was a step too far. Marianne explained to us that Florence had a feud with the

Fitzroys, but fancy taking it out on a young lad like that! I was horrified.'

'Perhaps one of the Fitzroys murdered Lady Florence?'

'In revenge for the punctured ball?'

'Possibly. But their disagreements were clearly deeper than that.'

'There was the business about buying Marianne's mother's house, wasn't there? I suspect there's much more to that feud than we know about.'

Duke swam in the sea, his black head bobbing confidently above the gentle waves. Rosie watched him cautiously from the shoreline.

'I've just remembered something else!' said Lottie. 'When we met Dr Blackwood here, there was something tense between him and Lady Florence.'

'You're right, Lottie, there was. I remember feeling uncomfortable at the time. He was in a cheery mood, but she wasn't saying much, was she? It's probably because she was angry he was trespassing on her beach. But maybe there was more to it than that?'

'He was quite familiar with her and called her Florence,' said Lottie. 'And she corrected him to address her as Lady Florence.'

'I remember. And didn't she describe him as insufferable? I asked if they had fallen out over something and she didn't want to say any more about it. There was something funny about that, Lottie.'

'And there's something else, too. Do you remember them briefly discussing the weather? He said it would get breezy the following day and predicted she would go for a sail.'

'And she confirmed she would. So Dr Blackwood was another one who knew, Lottie!'

Chapter Fifteen

'YOU NEED to catch this man at once, Detective!' said Rupert Cavendish. They sat on worn leather chairs in the empty lounge bar at the Star Hotel. Framed photographs of local fishing trawlers hung on the wall and the odour of stale beer and tobacco lingered in the air. 'You cannot allow someone to get away with murdering my wife!'

He put his pipe in his mouth and glared at Detective Lynton.

'When did you last see her, Lord Cavendish?'

'Yesterday afternoon. She was out when I called round, but I waited for her.'

'Why?'

'Because I wanted to talk to her! Can't a man talk to his wife?'

'Lady Cavendish was your former wife.'

'Yes, exactly. And Tidecrest House was once my home.'

'What time did you visit?'

'About three. And half an hour later, she returned from a picnic with her loud American friend.'

'And why did you visit Lady Cavendish?'

'I needed to speak to her about something.'

'And what was the conversation about?'

Rupert gritted his teeth. Detectives were a nosy bunch, and it was none of the chap's business. But he knew that if he showed any reluctance to answer his questions, then he was going to appear guilty.

'Personal matters, if I must be frank with you, Detective. It's a little embarrassing to have to discuss them with you here and now. And particularly difficult too, seeing as my former wife has been murdered. We may have been divorced, but I still held a great affection for her. We were married for twenty-five years.'

'I realise this must be very upsetting for you, my lord. And while I understand you don't wish to disclose the details of your conversation, I'm going to have to ask you for them all the same. We've got a murderer to catch.'

'But it won't help you at all with catching the murderer who's running around out there!' Rupert sucked on his pipe, then removed it from his mouth. 'But I shall comply with your request, Detective, because I'm a good man. Hopefully, it won't take up too much of your time, so you can get back out there and find the killer. Now, if you must know what we discussed, my wife and I were discussing a reconciliation.'

'You discussed getting back together again after your divorce?'

'Yes. We were in the early and delicate stages of negotiating it all. I can't really tell you anything more than that.'

'I hear you were disappointed by the outcome of your conversation on the terrace.'

Rupert laughed. 'I expect Marianne Trent told you that, didn't she? She always took my wife's side in arguments. Don't believe a word she tells you.'

'Who suggested the idea of a reconciliation?'

Rupert puffed up his chest, reluctant to admit to such

weakness. 'My wife suggested it,' he said. 'I've recently returned from America and I had some business to attend to in the area. We happened to bump into one another here in Fernwood. To be honest with you, Detective, I think the mere sight of me reminded her of what she'd lost. And like I said, I was still fond of Florence. So I called on her a few times and we got on well.'

'Were there any disagreements between you?'

'None whatsoever. We used to have disagreements all the time, that was why we got divorced. But between you and me, Detective, my break in America seemed to work wonders. Being reunited helped us appreciate each other again. She realised how much she'd missed me, and I realised how much I'd missed her.'

'Did you discuss moving back into Tidecrest House?'

'Absolutely. She was very keen on the idea. As was I. So we broadly agreed that's what would happen. Then someone went and did this to her. It was as if they wished to ruin any chance we had of being happy together.'

'Do you know of anybody who would wish to do that?'

'No, I can't think of anybody who wished to stop us from reconciling. And besides, who knows what the motive was for murdering my wife? I can't think of anyone who would have wished to harm her. She was well-liked. I would add that she never exchanged a cross word with anyone, but that would be a lie, Detective.'

Chapter Sixteen

'WHO DID Lady Cavendish exchange cross words with?' asked Detective Lynton.

Rupert shifted in his seat, explaining Florence's rudeness was tricky. 'Before I reply, Detective, you must understand a little about my wife's character. In fact, as a local man, I'm sure you knew her quite well yourself. There was no doubt she was direct in the manner she spoke to people. She didn't suffer fools gladly. As a result, some sensitive types were easily offended. I'm sure you know the ones.'

'I don't think I do.'

'Alright then, I can see you're expecting me to spit it out. The Fitzroy family. We had some disagreements with them over the years because they're cantankerous. They like to pretend they do many valuable and useful things in our community. And they're good at presenting themselves as well-meaning people. But if you know them well, Detective, you'll know it's all an act. But has one of them murdered my wife? I simply couldn't tell you. And it's not my job to point the finger, either. You'll need to get yourself over to Fairhaven Manor and speak to them, Detective. And I advise you to do so. I'm not accusing any of them of murder, but I think it's probably worth your while having a discussion with them all the same.'

'Anyone else your former wife had cross words with?'

'Only the other sensitive types, Detective. And Fernwood seems to have its fair share of those.'

Rupert didn't like the way Detective Lynton looked at him. His eyes scrutinised him as he spoke, as if searching for signs of deceit. But Rupert was the cleverer one. He was descended from generations of the landed gentry. It would take much more than a rural policeman to unsettle him.

'What time did you leave your former home yesterday, Lord Cavendish?'

'Well, let me see now. I got there at about three o'clock. Then Florence turned up at half-past three. We had a discussion on the terrace. A short discussion, I should add, because she had the loud American woman with her. And then I departed shortly after that. I would say I left about twenty-to-four. A quarter to at the latest.'

'And where did you go then?'

'I came back here.'

'And how did you get here?'

'I took a leisurely walk, so it was probably about half-past four when I got here.'

'Did anyone at the hotel see you here?'

'Of course. They must have done. The chap behind the desk. I must have passed some people on the stairs or in the corridor too.'

'Anyone you particularly remember who we can ask for an alibi?'

Rupert felt a snap of irritation. 'Now, just a moment. An alibi, Detective? Why do I need an alibi?'

'It's simply routine, Lord Cavendish. We need to establish

exactly where everyone was at the time of your former wife's death.'

'And if you come across someone who can't establish where they were, what are they then? A suspect?'

'It's the standard method of carrying out an inquiry, Lord Cavendish. I realise you might find the request offensive, but it doesn't mean you're a suspect. It's just something we need to establish with absolutely everybody who saw Lady Florence yesterday. I'm sure you understand.'

'Very well. Like I say, the hotel staff here would have seen me. You can't miss a chap like me in a little hotel like this.'

'Who can we ask specifically?'

'The staff! Just ask around in here. I don't understand why you're making a meal of this.' Rupert felt sure someone would claim to have seen him around.

'May I ask how you spent the rest of your evening, Lord Cavendish?'

'Well yes, it was quite simple. I put my feet up for a bit, then I changed for dinner. I came down to this bar for a drink. There wasn't a lot of atmosphere, but that's often the case in establishments like this. And then I dined alone in the dining room. Practically every staff member in this hotel would have seen me there. Then I retired early for the night.' Rupert realised he hadn't yet appeared distressed by his wife's death. He gave a sniff, as if struggling to speak. Then he uttered a few more words. 'Little did I know I would wake up the following morning to the worst news in the world!'

Chapter Seventeen

'I DON'T UNDERSTAND who could have done this to Lady Florence,' said Miss Trent. She twisted a handkerchief around her fingers as she sat with Lottie, Rosie and Mrs Moore in the sitting room. 'If I'm really forced to consider it, then I suppose Lord Cavendish is the most likely suspect. She said no to his request for a reconciliation.'

'He did look very disappointed about it,' said Mrs Moore.

'Perhaps the disappointment turned to anger as he began to walk back to the village,' said Miss Trent. 'Then maybe he came back to speak to her a second time, and it escalated into... Oh, I can't bear to think about it!'

'I've met Lord Cavendish a few times,' said Mrs Moore. 'But I don't know him very well. Would you say he had the character to do something so dreadful?'

'No, I wouldn't. He has a temper. But that's not unusual, is it? Lots of people have a temper, but they don't murder people. And I've never known him to lash out or be violent towards anyone. That would seem out of character.'

'And if Lord Cavendish had wished to speak to Lady Florence a second time yesterday, he would have come back to the house, wouldn't he?' said Mrs Moore. 'And none of us saw him again that evening.'

'Unless he saw Lady Florence walking to the boathouse,' said Lottie. 'He may have joined her then.'

'And then the pair went into the boathouse to continue their conversation? It's possible, isn't it?' said Mrs Moore. 'He might have wanted to speak to her in private instead of having the three of us present.'

'But I can't believe he murdered her,' said Miss Trent, 'even though he seems the most likely suspect. And now I don't know what to think about Lord Cavendish. I don't know whether to feel sorry for him or feel angry at him.'

'We know Lord Cavendish wanted to live in this house again,' said Lottie. 'Would the estate have passed to him after her death?'

'No,' said Miss Trent.

'You've raised an interesting point, Lottie!' said Mrs Moore. 'Who sets to benefit from Lady Florence's death?'

'It's me,' said Miss Trent.

Lottie felt her jaw drop at this news, then the butler entered the room. 'Dr Blackwood is here, Miss Trent. May I show him in?'

'Dr Blackwood?' Miss Trent smoothed her wavy hair. 'Very well, Smith. We're ready.'

The growling terrier arrived first. Rosie huddled up to Lottie's skirt and Duke the labrador hid behind an armchair.

'Oh Brutus, stop being so grumpy,' said Edward Blackwood as he strode into the room. He wore a dark morning suit and his grey hair was neatly combed. He paused and gave a considerate bow. 'Please accept my deepest condolences, Miss Trent.'

'Thank you, Dr Blackwood.'

'And my condolences to you too, Mrs Moore. And you too, Miss Sprigg.'

They both thanked him.

'I hope I'm not interrupting,' he said.

'No, of course not, Dr Blackwood,' said Miss Trent. 'Do please join us.'

He sank into an armchair and summoned Brutus to his side. 'I'm in complete shock about the death of Lady Florence, and... I really don't know what else to say.'

'You don't have to say anything else,' said Miss Trent. 'Simply calling in and expressing your condolences is enough. I can only hope the police get hold of this man soon.'

'Man? How do you know it was a man?'

'I'm just assuming it was,' said Miss Trent. 'I couldn't imagine a woman committing such a dreadful act.'

'Women can be murderous too, you know, Marianne. I mean, Miss Trent.'

'Yes, I suppose they can be. But they're far more likely to use poison, aren't they? To actually hit poor Lady Florence over the head with a wrench like that...' She shuddered. 'I really can't bear to think about it.'

'Don't dwell on it, Miss Trent. It's a dreadful thought,' said Dr Blackwood. 'We must leave it to the police. Is there any word on how their investigation is progressing?'

'Not yet. I expect Detective Lynton is very busy speaking to everyone.'

'I have some information which might be useful to him.'

'What information is that, Dr Blackwood?' asked Miss Trent.

'I went for a walk out to Shipwreck Point yesterday. And I'm afraid to say I completely disobeyed Lady Florence and took a shortcut across her beach again. Both there and back.'

'Oh, Dr Blackwood, she told you not to!'

'I know, I know. I'm afraid there are a couple of reasons I like to walk across the beach. The first being that it's simply quicker than taking the route inland along the road. It removes about half a mile from the walk. And secondly, it's a much nicer stroll. I'd rather be walking along the beach than on the road where there's a risk of being flattened by one of Farmer Tussock's tractors. And I'm afraid there is another reason too.' He glanced down at the floor sadly.

'And what reason is that, Dr Blackwood?' asked Mrs Moore.

'I used to take the shortcut along the beach because I hoped I might bump into her.'

'Lady Florence, you mean?'

'I'm afraid so.' He sniffed, then pinched the bridge of his nose as if trying to contain his emotion.

Chapter Eighteen

'I'M ashamed to admit it, Mrs Moore, but I suppose it will come out soon enough,' said Dr Blackwood. 'Lady Florence and I had a brief liaison last Christmas. It was a passionate affair, yet short-lived. Florence ended it and I don't believe I've fully recovered yet.'

'She broke your heart, Dr Blackwood?'

'She did indeed.'

Lottie realised now why Lady Florence hadn't wished to explain to Mrs Moore why she and Dr Blackwood had fallen out.

'We kept our liaison secret at the time,' continued the doctor. 'And that's because I'm... oh dear, you shall judge me terribly for this.'

'For what?'

'I'm a married man. But in name only! My wife and I barely speak.'

'I see.'

'So it's a rather delicate situation, as I'm sure you can appreciate.'

Lottie noticed Miss Trent's expression was stony.

'Yes, that sounds like a delicate situation,' said Mrs Moore.

'And so I sometimes took a stroll over this way, in the hope I might see Florence again.'

'Even though she'd asked you not to walk on her beach?'

'Yes. I just wanted to see her. And having her tell me off for walking on her beach was better than not seeing her at all. Doesn't it sound silly?'

'It does a little.'

'And now she's gone... It's too upsetting for words.'

Miss Trent cleared her throat. 'What information do you have for the police, Dr Blackwood?'

'Ah yes, that. On my walk back from Shipwreck Point yesterday, I trespassed on the beach and saw something which puzzled me.'

'What?' asked Miss Trent.

'A rowing boat. It had been pulled up onto the beach. Brutus sniffed it, and I had a look at it. There were two oars inside it and I have no idea what it was doing there.'

'What time was this?' asked Mrs Moore.

'About seven o'clock, I think. The boat hadn't been there on my way out to Shipwreck Point. That was probably about quarter-past six. I remember thinking that if the boat belonged to Lady Florence, then she would have put it in her boathouse.'

'You must tell the police about this!' said Miss Trent. 'That rowing boat could belong to the murderer!'

'Would a murderer really row along the bay just to murder Lady Florence?' said Dr Blackwood.

'Of course,' said Miss Trent. 'It would have saved him the trouble of walking on Lady Florence's land. And, by visiting Lady Florence in that way, he escaped the attention of anyone at the house.'

'So it was quite sneaky when you think about it,' said Mrs Moore.

'But if it was someone visiting Lady Florence at the boathouse,' said Lottie, 'how did they know she would be there?'

'That's an excellent point, Lottie,' said Mrs Moore. 'It must have been someone who knew she was planning to go sailing.'

'Or a member of staff here at the house tipped them off,' said Miss Trent.

'But if a member of staff tipped them off,' said Lottie, 'that suggests more than one person could have been behind this.'

'Yes,' said Mrs Moore. 'That's something to consider, isn't it? A member of Lady Florence's household colluding with the murderer.'

'I refuse to believe someone in this household could have harmed her,' said Miss Trent. 'Everybody here is devastated by what's happened to her. I really don't see why they would have told a murderer about her plans to go sailing.'

'But maybe they didn't know the person they told was going to murder Lady Florence,' said Mrs Moore. 'I'm sure they had no idea what the owner of the rowing boat was planning. Surely they would have informed the police if they had.'

'And if that's the case,' said Lottie. 'Why hasn't that member of staff told the police about it now?'

'Because they're too scared,' said Mrs Moore. 'They could know the identity of the murderer, but they're too scared to tell the police because they might be accused of colluding with the murderer. Or because they're worried the murderer will come for them next.'

'A very valid concern,' said Dr Blackwood.

'Maybe Lady Florence agreed to meet the owner of the rowing boat,' said Lottie.

'Now, there's a thought,' said Mrs Moore. 'Perhaps they

planned to meet at seven, and then the person chose to murder her.'

Miss Trent shook her head. 'If Lady Florence had arranged to meet someone on the beach yesterday evening, she would have told me about it. She never hid anything from me.'

'Well, I shall tell the police about the rowing boat,' said Dr Blackwood, getting to his feet. 'And we can see what they make of it. After all, it's their job to solve this. There's nothing any of us can do but hope this barbaric individual is caught as soon as possible.'

Chapter Nineteen

BEFORE DINNER THAT EVENING, Lottie tried to continue the letter to Miss Holmes. 'This is what I've written so far, Rosie. "Dear Miss Holmes, Thank you very much for your letter." Now what shall I put next? Mrs Moore suggested it could be a chatty letter. But I don't know what to be chatty about. Perhaps I could tell her I'm currently staying by the sea?'

A knock at the door interrupted her. It was Mrs Moore.

'Would you mind doing up the zip of my dress, Lottie? I can't manage it.' As Lottie did so, Mrs Moore continued, 'It was interesting to hear about the rowing boat Dr Blackwood saw on the beach, wasn't it?'

'It was very interesting,' said Lottie. 'Hopefully, he's told Detective Lynton about it now. And it also proves something else.'

'Which is what?'

'It proves Dr Blackwood was near the boathouse at the time of Lady Florence's murder.'

Mrs Moore gasped. 'Of course! Why didn't I think of that, Lottie?' then she thought for a moment. 'But if he was happy to tell us he was there, it means he couldn't be the murderer. If he'd murdered Lady Florence, then he wouldn't wish to mention he had seen the rowing boat on the beach.'

'Perhaps there wasn't a rowing boat on the beach,' said Lottie. 'Perhaps Dr Blackwood can't prove he was elsewhere at that time, so he has to admit he was there and come up with the sighting of the rowing boat to throw people off the scent.'

'Good grief, Lottie. Do you think he could be that cunning?'

'It's possible. We know he's used to lying because he must have lied to his wife to cover up his secret affair with Lady Florence.'

'I don't condone adultery,' said Mrs Moore. 'But we can't make the assumption he's a murderer because his morals lapsed a little.'

'But he was keen to tell us about the rowing boat, wasn't he? I realise he called in to pass on his condolences. But perhaps he also wanted to put the idea of the boat into our heads as soon as possible.'

'And hoped no one would therefore suspect him. Goodness me, Lottie. For someone so young, you possess quite an ability to analyse people's motivations. Then again, it's possible that everything he told us is completely true and we should take him at his word. I'd like to think that, because I quite like Dr Blackwood. Although I have learned, unfortunately, that murderers can be likeable.'

Chapter Twenty

Lottie, Rosie and Mrs Moore went for a stroll around Fernwood-on-Sea the following morning.

'It's difficult to know what to do with oneself at times like this, isn't it, Lottie? I feel like we should stay here for the time being to support Miss Trent. But it feels awkward just sitting around in the house all day, doesn't it? I hope she's not offended we've gone out for a walk. I can't get used to the idea she's now the lady of Tidecrest House. Isn't it astonishing that Florence left everything to her?'

'Who else could she have left her estate to?' said Lottie.

'Well I suppose there could be a distant cousin. Or a niece or nephew perhaps. But Miss Trent has clearly served her well over the years and Florence decided to reward her loyalty.'

They walked along a cobbled street which ran parallel to the harbour. It was lined with little shops with colourful signs and awnings.

A shout from the doorway of an inn disturbed the peace. 'We're not open yet!' hollered a man. 'And when we do open, you're not allowed in!'

Lottie, Rosie and Mrs Moore stopped as a young man was hurled from the doorway into the street. The thick-armed man who'd thrown him went into the inn and slammed the door shut.

The red-faced young man stumbled to his feet before stooping to retrieve his cap from the cobbles.

'Good morning,' he muttered to them before he staggered on his way.

'Good grief,' said Mrs Moore. 'That's not very pleasant, is it? Now I recall visiting a lovely dress shop the last time I was here.' She pulled out her lorgnette and surveyed the street. 'Oh, it's still there! Come along, Lottie. Let's have a look inside.'

The shop was called Fernwood Fashions and had several elegant mannequins in the window. They wore stylish, low-waisted silk dresses in pastel shades.

Rosie waited outside while they went into the shop. Mrs Moore asked the shop assistant if they stocked any ankle-length dresses while Lottie tried on a few hats in front of a mirror.

A dark-haired lady arrived in the shop. 'Good morning, Laura,' she said, without appearing to notice Laura was already with a customer. 'I'm going up to London next week for the Wimbledon Tennis Tournament. I need five new outfits for it and I fear I've left it a little late.' She stopped when she noticed Mrs Moore with the shop assistant. 'Oh, hello,' she said stonily. 'I didn't realise I was interrupting.'

Mrs Moore smiled. 'Good morning,' she said. 'I believe we met briefly on Windy Edge the other day. Mrs Fitzroy, isn't it?'

'Yes, that's right.'

'I'm Mrs Moore and it's a pleasure to meet you properly. How's your son faring? He must have been very upset after Lady Florence deflated his ball.'

'He was extremely upset,' said Mrs Fitzroy. 'I was

saddened to hear about Lady Florence's death. And I don't like to speak ill of the deceased. However, it was dreadfully unreasonable of her.' She gave a sniff. 'My son has a new ball now and I think he's largely forgotten about the incident.'

'Did you not get along with Lady Florence?' asked Mrs Moore, clearly feigning ignorance.

'No. She was a snob, I'm afraid, and terribly rude. She considered herself superior to everyone else and had little to do with most people in the village. All she did was go out in her boat and shout at anyone who dared set foot on the beach.'

'She told me it was her private beach.'

'That may be so. But when a prominent member of the community owns such a beautiful natural asset, isn't it fair they should allow local people to enjoy it too? We own a substantial number of acres at Fairhaven Manor, but we allow people to walk through our estate so they can enjoy the beautiful landscape. I believe it's a duty of the privileged and wealthy to share the things they've been blessed with. I told Lady Florence that many times, but you won't be surprised to hear she didn't agree with me.'

'Is it fair to say she didn't have many friends locally?'

'Yes. She was rude and aloof. It wasn't quite so bad when Lord Cavendish was still at the house. He made a little more effort with the locals. But once he went off to America, she had little to do with anybody. So although it's sad she's no longer with us and died in such a horrible way, I'm afraid you won't find many people in the village who have much sympathy, Mrs Moore.'

'That is sad to hear indeed.'

'May I ask how you knew her?'

'I met her and Lord Cavendish ten years ago while skiing in the Alps. I found her quite delightful back then. It's a shame to hear she became so grumpy over the years.'

'Yes, it was a dreadful shame,' said Mrs Fitzroy. There was

a pause for a moment, and then she sighed. 'It could have been very different, indeed.'

'Do you mind if I ask what you mean by that?'

'Oh, I didn't mean anything by it.' She flicked her hand dismissively. 'I need something for Wimbledon, Laura!'

Chapter Twenty-One

MRS MOORE TOLD Miss Trent about the encounter with Victoria Fitzroy when they returned to Tidecrest House.

'I expect the Fitzroy family are laughing now,' said Miss Trent bitterly.

'I didn't get that impression, Marianne,' said Mrs Moore. 'Mrs Fitzroy seemed genuinely saddened about Lady Florence's death. Why do you think they could be laughing? Do you think they could be behind it?'

'I think they could be,' said Miss Trent. 'I can imagine Victoria Fitzroy getting very upset about Lady Florence deflating her son's football.'

'Enough to murder her?'

'I think so. From what I've heard, that family is capable of anything.'

'Really?'

'That rowing boat could have belonged to Victoria Fitzroy.'

'Does she have a rowing boat?'

'I don't know.'

A knock on the sitting-room window interrupted them. They turned to see Arthur Harris there.

Miss Trent got up and opened the window. 'What is it, Arthur?'

He removed his cap from his bald head. 'I just had that Detective Lynton asking me questions.'

'Yes, he's speaking to lots of people, Arthur.'

'Has he spoken to you yet?'

'A few times.'

'He asked me for an alibi!'

'I'm afraid that's to be expected.'

'How could he think I'd hurt Lady Florence like that?'

'He doesn't think you did, Arthur. He's asking everyone for an alibi.'

'I was at home. My wife can tell him that.'

'Good, then you have nothing to worry about.'

Arthur nodded and replaced his cap. 'Thank you, Miss Trent.'

He went on his way and Miss Trent closed the window. 'Poor Arthur,' she said. 'Things haven't been easy for him recently. The trouble with his son and now this.'

'What sort of trouble with his son?' asked Mrs Moore.

'He doesn't like discussing it, it's an embarrassment to him.' Miss Trent sat down and lowered her voice. 'So please don't tell him I've told you. But Arthur's son, Tom, has turned to drink. He's lost his job, he's left his wife, and all he does is drink and get thrown out of the village pubs. But I think he's been banned from most of them. But he keeps trying to return.'

Lottie thought of the young man they'd seen being thrown out of the inn earlier. She wondered if he had been Arthur's son.

'How sad,' said Mrs Moore. 'It must be a big worry for Arthur and his wife.'

'It is. They've taken in their daughter-in-law and the children. But they only have a small cottage, so it's a tight squeeze.'

'That's terrible,' said Mrs Moore. 'Once the drink gets hold of someone... well, it's very difficult to recover from. I speak from experience. One of my husbands was a drinker.'

'I'm sorry to hear it, Mrs Moore.'

'There's not a great deal you can do about it. And sometimes when people get into that state, they can become very selfish and unpleasant. They can be difficult to be around.'

'Yes, I think that's what Arthur has discovered, so he's in a quandary. The salary which he earns now has to support his wife, daughter-in-law, and four grandchildren. His son is incapable of working at the moment.'

'Awful.'

'I think I can make some provision for them with the money I've inherited from Lady Florence. I might be able to help them rent a larger cottage.'

'What a lovely thought, Miss Trent.'

'I could give Arthur a little pay rise. And I could offer to employ his son, Tom, but... well, he was working as a waiter at the seafood restaurant in the harbour, but they let him go. He couldn't find a job anywhere else after that.'

'Oh dear. I can only hope the young man manages to pull himself together again. Hopefully, he can stop his drinking, find work and support his family again. Then Arthur wouldn't have to do it.'

'That would be the best outcome,' said Miss Trent. 'We live in hope.' She glanced at the clock on the mantelpiece. 'Oh look at the time. I'd better get going. I have some errands to do in the village.'

Chapter Twenty-Two

'SO YOU'RE TELLING me you saw a rowing boat on Lady Florence's beach on the evening she was murdered?' asked Detective Lynton.

'That's right,' said Dr Edward Blackwood. He leant on the wooden counter of Fernwood-on-Sea police station.

'And when was this?'

'About seven. It could have been a little before or after that, I didn't check my watch at the time. I remember arriving home at about half-past seven.'

'Did you see anyone?'

Edward looked Detective Lynton in the eye. He had to be as convincing as possible. 'Absolutely no one,' he said. 'No one at all.'

'Did you hear anyone? Voices from inside the boathouse?'

'No. I didn't hear a thing.'

'And what did you think when you saw the boat?'

'I assumed it was someone visiting Lady Florence. And I thought no more of it.'

'Have you seen the rowing boat on that beach before?'

'No, I don't think so.'

'And what did the rowing boat look like?'

Edward couldn't resist a laugh. 'It looked like any other rowing boat! It was made of wood, it had some planks in it for seats, and there were a couple of oars resting in it.'

'Anything to make it distinguishable from other rowing boats?' asked the detective. 'Did you notice it had a name on it? Had it been painted a particular colour?'

'No. It was a completely ordinary rowing boat.'

'So you wouldn't be able to identify that particular rowing boat if you saw it again?'

'Are you planning a rowing boat identity parade, Detective?' His joke was met with a frown. Edward gave a little cough of embarrassment and continued. 'I suppose I would know it if I saw it on the beach again. But if it was placed next to another equally plain rowing boat, then I would probably struggle to tell the two apart. I'm afraid I can't give you any clues about who owned that boat, Detective. I'm just merely telling you what I saw.'

'You say you took a walk out to Shipwreck Point and back. Did you see anyone else on your walk?'

'I saw an old man on the path out at Shipwreck Point. I often see him and say hello. I've no idea who he is though. I don't know them by name. Just people I nod and say hello to when I'm out walking that way. But I didn't see anyone else on the walk outside of Fernwood.'

'Did you see Lady Florence at all?'

'Not during that walk, no.'

'Did you call in at the boathouse when you passed it?'

'No. Why would I have done that?'

The detective stroked his tidy, steel-grey moustache. 'I understand you were friendly with Lady Florence. Perhaps you saw the rowing boat and wondered if that meant she was close by in the boathouse?'

How did the detective know about him and Florence? 'No, I didn't think that,' he said.

'Could you tell me a little more about your friendship with Lady Florence?'

Edward sighed. It was the last thing he wished to be asked about. He was regretting visiting the police station to tell him about the rowing boat. 'There's very little to tell, Detective. Lady Florence and I enjoyed each other's company last Christmas, but then she decided to put a stop to it.'

'Were you upset by that?'

'Upset? Goodness, no!' He smiled to cover up his lie. 'It wasn't serious between us. We were two mature people who had lived life a little, and we enjoyed each other's companionship for a brief time. There's little more to say.'

'Did you see Lady Florence after she put a stop to it?'

'Yes. It was difficult not to. I like to walk my dog out to Shipwreck Point and that means passing her property.'

'You chose to walk along her beach. Even though it's private property.'

'Yes, I admit that. It's a quicker, nicer route to take. And because I once knew Florence well, I thought she didn't mind.'

'And did she mind?'

'Well, of course she did. That was Lady Florence for you. You know yourself what she was like. But her bark was much worse than her bite.'

'When was the last time you saw Lady Florence?'

'Why are you asking me all these questions, Detective? I only came in here to tell you about the rowing boat. And I'm regretting it now.'

'I'd have caught up with you one way or another, Dr Blackwood. You were on my list of people to speak to.'

'Was I?' He tried to shrug off the uncomfortable sensation this remark gave him. 'I saw her the day before she died. And she told me off for walking on her beach again. She was with the American woman and her assistant.'

'You had a conversation?'

'Of sorts. As I've said, she told me to get off her beach. We exchanged a few words, she introduced me to her companions, then I continued my walk.'

'Can you think of anyone who wished to harm Lady Florence?'

'No! I realise she wasn't the most popular person in the village. But murder? That really was a step too far, Detective.' He pulled his handkerchief from his pocket. 'I shall miss her.'

Chapter Twenty-Three

LOTTIE, Rosie and Mrs Moore took a stroll around the garden in the sunshine. Duke cantered out to join them, and he and Rosie played together.

'Oh look, Arthur's over there,' said Mrs Moore. 'Let's have a chat with him.'

Arthur Harris was busy pruning faded flowers from a shrub with a pair of secateurs.

'Good afternoon, Arthur,' said Mrs Moore.

He pulled the cap from his head and gave her a bow. 'Mrs Moore.'

'Busy in the garden, I see.'

'Yes. Always busy.'

'I hope you don't mind me asking you a question, Arthur.'

'Not at all, Mrs Moore.'

'We've heard there was a rowing boat on the beach when Lady Florence was murdered. Do you recall seeing the boat there that evening?'

'I wasn't there at that time. I was at home.'

'Ah yes, of course. So you don't know who the rowing

boat could have belonged to?'

'No. Could have been anybody. There are a lot of folks about with boats. Someone visiting Lady Florence, perhaps. I never knew when she had visitors or not. That's the sort of thing Miss Trent and the household staff would know about.'

'Dr Blackwood claims he saw a rowing boat moored on the beach that evening.'

'If that's what he said, then it must be so. He's a man of his word.'

Lottie found Arthur's responses odd. Although he was answering Mrs Moore's questions, he was doing so in as few words as possible. She couldn't decide if his conversation was usually this limited, or whether he was hiding something.

'If Dr Blackwood was on the beach, then he was close to the boathouse at the time of Lady Florence's murder,' said Mrs Moore. 'And yet he doesn't appear to have heard or seen anything suspicious. Other than the boat.'

'I can't speak for Dr Blackwood. But I assume he's told the police all about it. We must leave it to them now.'

'Do you know Dr Blackwood well?'

'Quite well. He and Lady Florence were friendly for a while, but you didn't hear it from me. He's a respectable man who works hard. He would never have laid a finger on Lady Florence, and I won't hear a word otherwise.'

'Oh no, I don't believe he could have done that. He seems a pleasant chap. I'm sure he's told Detective Lynton all about the rowing boat and I can only hope the police find the owner. Can you think of anyone, Arthur, who would have wanted to harm Lady Florence?'

'I can't think of anyone, Mrs Moore. I know she wasn't popular with everyone, but I don't understand why someone would murder her.'

'Me neither. Well, thank you for chatting so frankly with

us, Arthur. I realise it can't be easy for you as you worked for Lady Florence for many years.'

'Indeed I did.'

'And I hope you don't mind, but Miss Trent told us a little about your family and how you're supporting them all. I'm terribly sorry about your troubles. I would like to help if possible.'

'That's very kind, Mrs Moore, but I don't accept charity.'

'Very well. If you change your mind, then just let me know.'

'I shan't. But thank you all the same, Mrs Moore. You're a good lady.'

Chapter Twenty-Four

Detective Lynton called at Tidecrest House while Miss Trent was still in the village.

'I'm afraid there's just me and Miss Sprigg here, Detective Lynton,' said Mrs Moore.

'You'll do for the time being.'

'Oh, thank you. Will you have some tea with us?'

'Thank you.'

They drank tea while sitting on the sunny terrace. Rosie and Duke played together on the lawn.

'So how's the investigation going, Detective?' asked Mrs Moore.

'I'm not used to a case like this. In my entire time working as a police officer in Fernwood-on-Sea, I've never had to deal with a murder.'

'No murder at all?'

'No. It's very rare around these parts. However, we're up to the task, so it's just a matter of sorting through all the information and trying to make sense of it.'

'Has Dr Blackwood told you about the rowing boat he saw on the beach?'

'Yes, he has.'

'And can you identify the owner of the rowing boat?'

'That's going to be quite a task. Rowing boats are quite popular around here, as you can probably imagine. Quite a lot of people use them to get about.'

'The rowing boat has to belong to the murderer, doesn't it?'

'We don't know, Mrs Moore. But my men are working hard on it.'

'And what about Lord Cavendish? Have you established where he was at the time of the murder?'

'We're still making inquiries with the hotel he's staying at. There's no doubt he was seen by members of staff at the hotel that evening. But we're trying to narrow down the sightings to exact times. It's quite tricky. Few of us are constantly looking at the clock, are we? And in a case like this, half an hour one way or another makes quite a difference. It can rule someone either in or out of the investigation.'

'So is Lord Cavendish in or out?'

The detective chuckled. 'You're trying to make me spill the beans, aren't you, Mrs Moore? At the moment, he's more out than in. A man of Lord Cavendish's standing couldn't possibly commit such a horrible murder. Particularly of his former wife, whom he loved and adored for so long. It's merely a matter of procedure to establish an alibi for him, and I'm sure we'll get that established.'

'So who does that leave?' asked Mrs Moore. 'The staff here at the house?'

'We've been considering them all, and it's quite clear everyone who works here respected Lady Florence a great deal. I can't find any reason why a member of her staff would have wanted to harm her. We've managed to establish alibis for practically all of them.'

'That's good news.'

'And for you and Miss Sprigg, a maid and a butler can vouch for the fact you were in the dining room here at the time of Lady Florence's murder.'

'Indeed we were. So it seems everyone in this household has been accounted for at the time of Lady Florence's murder.'

'Almost.' The detective scratched his moustache. 'There's only one person I can't find an alibi for.'

'Who's that?'

'Miss Trent.'

'That's quite easy, Detective. She was with us. Wasn't she Lottie?'

Lottie nodded.

'She was with you until seven,' said the detective. 'And then she says she went to Lady Florence's study to make a telephone call to her aunt. Her aunt wasn't available to speak, so she says she did some tidying in there.'

'That's right.'

'But I haven't yet found anyone who saw Miss Trent in the study.'

'Someone must have done. She was in there for an hour.'

'Was she in the study for an hour? Or was her time unaccounted for during that hour?'

'Oh,' said Mrs Moore. 'I see what you mean, Detective.'

'I came here to speak to her about it.' The detective drained his tea. 'But I shall come back tomorrow.'

Chapter Twenty-Five

'GOODNESS ME, LOTTIE,' said Mrs Moore, after the detective had left. 'Could Miss Trent really have murdered Florence?'

'I can't imagine it.'

'Me neither. But it doesn't look good, does it? She was dining with us, and then she abruptly went off to make her telephone call. I thought it was odd at the time.'

'I thought the same,' said Lottie. 'I thought the telephone call could have waited until she'd properly finished her meal. But she dashed off.'

'Perhaps she had made an arrangement with her aunt to speak to her at seven.'

'But there was no answer on the aunt's telephone. You'd have thought if they had arranged to speak at a certain time, then the aunt would have been there to answer.'

'Very true.'

'And stating there had been no answer is quite convenient for Miss Trent,' said Lottie. 'It means the aunt can't confirm whether or not the telephone call was made.'

'So it's possible Miss Trent didn't make the telephone call

80

after all? How interesting. And to then spend an hour tidying the study also seems like an odd thing to do. Oh, I feel terrible saying this, Lottie, but I think Miss Trent could be lying.'

'Miss Trent has presumably known for a while that she would inherit this estate,' said Lottie.

'Yes. So why murder Florence when she knew she was going to inherit the estate anyway?'

'Perhaps she got impatient. Or perhaps she was in need of the money?'

'I can't see why Miss Trent would have needed the money. She lived here in the house with Lady Florence and had few outgoings.'

'Few that we know of. She could have a terrible gambling habit which we don't know about,' said Lottie. 'Or maybe she needed the money to help someone in need. Her mother, perhaps?'

'But it seems her mother is comfortable in her cottage. Especially after Lady Florence bought it to stop Victoria Fitzroy from buying it and putting up the rent.'

Lottie thought for a moment. 'Perhaps she was being blackmailed.'

'Why would someone do that?'

'I don't know.'

'Me neither. I suppose we don't know Miss Trent very well, do we? I don't like suspecting her because she seems very nice and kind. But we don't know what secrets she's hiding, do we?'

Chapter Twenty-Six

'I BUMPED into Lady Florence's friend in Fernwood Fashions today,' said Victoria Fitzroy at dinner that evening. 'An American called Mrs Moore.'

'Did she seem upset about the murder?' asked Lady Fitzroy.

'I think so. It was difficult to tell. I don't think she actually knew her very well.'

'I still can't believe Lady Florence is dead and gone,' said Lord Fitzroy. 'She was the sort of lady one assumed would go on forever.'

'Nobody goes on forever, Harold,' said his wife.

'No, but some people seem like they will. I never liked the woman, but it's all terribly sad.'

'It's terribly worrying,' said Lady Fitzroy, putting down her knife and fork. 'We could be next!'

'I doubt it,' said Victoria. 'The crime was clearly committed by someone who wanted to harm Lady Florence. I should think everyone in this family is quite safe.'

'But how do you know that, Victoria? You can't be certain at all. We have no idea why Lady Florence was attacked like that. Perhaps someone is planning on bumping off all the landed gentry?'

'Just like the French Revolution all over again,' said Lord Fitzroy. 'But here instead of France. The Fernwood Revolution.'

'Oh don't, Harold,' said his wife. 'I find the thought completely terrifying!'

'There's no need to be terrified,' said Victoria. 'I'm sure we'll be fine.'

'And why do you feel so sure, Victoria?'

'Because I can't think of anyone who would wish to harm any of us. We've not upset anyone, and nobody dislikes us.'

'Well, that's true,' said Lord Fitzroy. 'We are quite popular, aren't we? We do so much good work for the village and its inhabitants. So Victoria has a point. I don't think we're unpopular enough to be murdered.'

'It may be nothing to do with being unpopular,' said Lady Fitzroy. 'There might be another motive entirely. Perhaps she was silenced.'

'Well, I've thought for many years that Lady Florence ought to be silenced,' said her husband. 'Not murdered, I should add. But just quietened down a bit. She had too much to say for herself.'

'I don't mean silence in that respect, Harold,' said Lady Fitzroy. 'I mean she was silenced because she knew someone's secret.'

'What secret?'

'I don't know. And she's been murdered now, so we'll never know. Or perhaps she was blackmailing someone.'

'I can't imagine Lady Florence blackmailing anyone,' said Victoria. 'She didn't need the money.'

'Even rich people can be greedy,' said Lady Fitzroy. 'All the money in the world isn't enough for some people. They still want more.'

'Lady Florence was many things,' said Victoria, 'but I don't believe she was a blackmailer.'

'It could have been a passion of the heart,' said Lord Fitzroy. 'Perhaps a lover killed her.'

'Don't talk like that, Harold. It's vulgar,' said Lady Fitzroy.

'But a perfectly valid motive. She was far more likely to have been murdered for that reason than blackmailing someone.'

'Well, there was talk of her and Dr Blackwood last Christmas,' said Victoria.

'Dr Blackwood?' said Lady Fitzroy.

'Yes. Did you not hear about it?'

'No I didn't. How scandalous! Dr Blackwood is a married man.'

'Dr Blackwood would never have done a thing like that,' said Lord Fitzroy, puffing out his chest. 'He's a fine, upstanding gentleman.'

'And a doctor,' said his wife.

'Obviously.'

A thought occurred to Victoria as she cut a piece of asparagus with her knife and fork. 'Our feud with Lady Florence won't have been forgotten by some people,' she said.

'And what do you mean by that, Victoria?' asked her father-in-law.

'Many people in the village have witnessed arguments between us and Lady Florence over the years. Some might assume that we'd had enough of her and decided to murder her.'

'Absolute nonsense!' said Lord Fitzroy. 'Absolutely nobody in the village would dare believe such a thing!'

'You'd be surprised. I've already heard some mutterings.'

'Mutterings? From whom?'

'I overheard two of the maids discussing it. Word has

spread how Lady Florence punctured Tarquin's football on Windy Edge the other day. Apparently, it's been suggested that someone in this family could have murdered her in revenge.'

'Over a punctured football?' said Lady Fitzroy. 'Ridiculous! Although I must admit I was so enraged when I discovered what had happened, that I was tempted to march over and push her off the cliff. What a cruel thing to do!'

'That's the sort of woman she was,' said Lord Fitzroy. 'So I suppose it's no great surprise that she's no longer around. Treat people like that on a daily basis and you end up paying the price.'

'Who gets Tidecrest House?' said Lady Fitzroy. 'Lord Cavendish?'

'No,' said Victoria. 'My hairdresser told me it's Marianne Trent.'

'Her companion? She gets the entire house?'

'Apparently so. Lady Florence wasn't going to leave it to her former husband, was she? I suppose she considered Miss Trent to be the person closest to her.'

'I can't quite get over the fact that Miss Trent will have that enormous great house,' said Lady Fitzroy. 'And to think all that fuss was made over the little cottage her mother lives in. Do you remember how Lady Florence paid too much for it just so you couldn't buy it, Victoria?'

'How could I forget?'

'Miss Trent will probably move her mother out of that cottage now and install her in the house. A pair of commoners. Little more than glorified maids. Can you imagine it? The world really isn't fair.'

Chapter Twenty-Seven

'DETECTIVE LYNTON HAS ASKED to interview me again today,' said Miss Trent at breakfast the following morning. 'I don't know why. I really can't think what else I can tell him!'

Lottie and Mrs Moore exchanged a glance.

'He probably wishes to clarify a few things,' said Mrs Moore.

'Such as what?' Miss Trent bit her lip anxiously. 'I've told him everything I know.'

'Oh, you know what detectives are like, Miss Trent. They've always got lots of questions.'

'It's making me feel like I've done something wrong!'

'Have you?'

'No!'

'Then I'm sure all will be fine, Miss Trent.'

An uncomfortable silence followed, and Lottie felt the need to speak. 'I'd like to walk out to Shipwreck Point today,' she said.

'That's a lovely walk,' said Miss Trent, seemingly relieved by the change in conversation. 'I would come with you, but I have to speak to the detective.'

'And I'd come with you too, Lottie,' said Mrs Moore. 'But it's a little too far for my liking.'

'It's about the same distance as the walk to Windy Edge,' said Miss Trent.

'Which is too far for my liking,' said Mrs Moore. 'I'll stay here.' She turned to Lottie. 'It's another warm day. Make sure you take a flask of lemonade with you.'

Lottie and Rosie set off after breakfast. They walked down to the beach and Rosie trotted up to the waves. She played in the shallow water as Lottie headed for the wooded path at the end of the bay.

The only sound was the wash of waves on the shore. Lottie felt a shiver as she reached the boathouse. It was closed up and silent.

She paused for a moment on the beach and wondered if anyone standing in this same spot would have heard Lady Florence and her murderer in the boathouse.

Had there been an argument? Had Lady Florence cried out? The attack itself would surely have created a noise. Lottie wondered how Dr Blackwood had been here at the time, yet claimed he'd seen and heard nothing.

It was possible he was lying.

Lottie whistled to Rosie and swiftly walked on, keen to get away.

The path led uphill through a wooded area before opening out onto a grassy route along the clifftop. Lottie could see the silhouette of the little church in the distance. Keen to keep Rosie away from the cliff edge, Lottie attached the lead to her collar and kept her close.

It was a sunny day with a warm breeze. Sunlight shimmered on the sea and a sail boat was dwarfed by the expanse of blue. Birds chirped in the small weather-beaten trees which did their best to grow in this exposed place. The crash of waves drifted up from the rocks at the foot of the cliff. On a warm summer's day, it was beautiful here. But Lottie could imagine it being very bleak when a storm came in.

She paused to look at the view behind her. Tidecrest House was clearly visible in its proud position above the sea. Beyond it lay Fernwood-on-Sea with its pretty harbour. It was a scene perfect enough for a postcard. But lurking within it somewhere was a murderer.

Lottie shuddered and resumed her walk to Shipwreck Point. She could see the church more clearly now. It was an ancient stone building with a stocky tower and a tumbledown wall enclosing a small graveyard. She and Rosie soon reached the gate which led into the churchyard. The long grass was filled with colourful wildflowers. Age had caused the headstones to sink and lean at precarious angles. They were covered with lichen, and Lottie found it difficult to decipher many of the inscriptions.

She rested on an old wooden bench by the side of the church and took some sips from her flask of lemonade. Rosie jumped up onto the bench next to her and the pair enjoyed the solitude for a moment.

'It feels nice to be away from Tidecrest House, doesn't it, Rosie? It's lovely to get some peace. Just a moment, who's this?'

Two distant figures were walking along the clifftop path towards her. They were accompanied by a dog.

'I'm not in the mood to make polite conversation. How about you, Rosie?'

The corgi looked back at her with her large dark eyes.

'I'll assume that's a no. Let's look inside the church. It will be a lot cooler in there too.'

Chapter Twenty-Eight

THE HEAVY CHURCH door creaked as Lottie pushed it open, then she and Rosie stepped into the chilly interior. It had an old, earthy smell. Colourful rays of sunlight shone through a stained glass window at the far end. Once Lottie's eyes had adjusted to the gloom, she could see five rows of pews facing a little altar below the window. Stone plaques on the walls commemorated ships which had been wrecked on the rocks of the headland. Lottie was reading about a ship called The Unity wrecked in the 1770s when she heard voices.

They came from a narrow window set in the wall of the church. Lottie recalled seeing it when she had sat on the bench. She realised the two figures she had seen were now sitting on the same bench.

Lottie stepped closer to the window and listened.

'We don't want to give him every little piece of information from that evening, because he'll be distracted by it,' said a man's voice. 'He'll waste his time on it instead of actually finding the person who did this.'

The voice sounded like Dr Blackwood.

Then the other voice spoke, 'I agree with that.'

'Excellent. I knew I could trust you. You're a good man, Arthur.'

Lottie looked down at Rosie who sat by her feet. 'Edward Blackwood and Arthur Harris!' she mouthed to her dog.

'Your secret's safe with me, Dr Blackwood.'

Lottie held her breath, hoping to hear more. But there was a pause in the conversation. 'Middlesex batted well yesterday, didn't they?' said Dr Blackwood.

The conversation had turned to cricket. Lottie sighed and sat down on a pew. If she left the church now, the two men would see her and wonder if she'd overheard their conversation. She decided it would be best to wait for them to leave before she walked back to Tidecrest House.

While she waited, Lottie tried to work out what their conversation had been about. Who was the man they'd been discussing, could it be Detective Lynton? And what was Dr Blackwood's secret?

Chapter Twenty-Nine

LOTTIE AND ROSIE didn't have to wait long in the church. After discussing the cricket, Dr Blackwood announced he had a patient to see, and the two men left the bench.

Lottie pushed open the church door and saw the two figures and the dog walking back to the bay. She waited until they were distant specks before she followed.

As they made their way along the clifftop path, Lottie spotted a few boats in the bay. Some had gleaming white triangles for their sails, while another was larger with a smoky funnel. Then Lottie spotted a tiny little boat with no funnel or sail at all.

A rowing boat.

It was being rowed towards the harbour and was too far away for Lottie to identify the occupant.

'I wish I had a telescope or pair of binoculars,' she said to Rosie. 'I want to see who's in that boat. Let's follow it.'

She jogged down the path to the little patch of woodland at the edge of the bay. When she reached the beach, the rowing boat was still within sight.

Lottie kept her eye on the boat as they walked along the

beach. Eventually, she reached the steps at the harbour wall and climbed up. Then she walked along the harbour wall a little and watched the boat approach.

As it drew closer, she could see the man rowing it. He had a large grey beard and wore a fisherman's smock.

'It's the man who waved at Lady Florence from his boat the other day,' Lottie said to Rosie. 'Captain O'Malley.'

The rowing boat entered the harbour, and the captain rowed it deftly to where The Golden Herring was moored.

'I wonder,' Lottie said to Rosie. 'Could it have been Captain O'Malley's rowing boat on the beach the other evening?'

Chapter Thirty

LOTTIE HAD a lot to discuss with Mrs Moore when she returned to Tidecrest House. They spoke in the privacy of Mrs Moore's room where Lottie hoped no one could overhear.

'Dr Blackwood has a secret?' said Mrs Moore. 'What could it be?'

'Something which Arthur Harris has found out and has promised not to tell,' said Lottie. 'They're clearly colluding about something because Dr Blackwood said he didn't want to give Detective Lynton every little piece of information from that evening because he'd be distracted by it.'

'Can you be sure he was talking about the detective?'

'No. He didn't mention him by name. But I think he must have been referring to him.'

'So Dr Blackwood and Arthur know something about that evening which they haven't told the police,' said Mrs Moore. 'Interesting. And you think it could have been Captain O'Malley's boat which Dr Blackwood saw on the beach?'

'I don't know. It's a possibility. And do you remember

seeing him in the harbour when we were there with Lady Florence? He gave her a friendly wave, but she didn't seem to want to acknowledge him.'

'Yes, that was odd.' Mrs Moore gave a sigh. 'Marianne will know more about Captain O'Malley, but I'm wary about asking her. To be honest, Lottie,' she lowered her voice to a whisper, 'I don't trust her. Maybe it's unreasonable of me to think this, but I think she's suspicious. Her whereabouts at the time of Lady Florence's death are questionable, aren't they?'

Lottie nodded.

'So as for Captain O'Malley, let's speak to him ourselves, shall we?'

'And ask him what?'

'All sorts of things. I'll just pretend to be a nosy American tourist, and maybe he'll be happy to chat to me. Come along Lottie, let's go and find him.'

They set off and arrived at the harbour about fifteen minutes later. Lottie pointed out where The Golden Herring was moored. They walked along the harbour wall towards it.

'Do you think he's on board, Lottie?'

'It's difficult to know.'

They stopped near the old fishing trawler. 'Yoo-hoo!' called out Mrs Moore. The noise startled Lottie so much that her feet left the ground. 'I say!' called out Mrs Moore. 'Hello?'

There was a scrabbling noise as a head emerged from the dirty white cabin. It was the bushy-bearded head of Captain O'Malley.

'What on earth?' he said.

'Good afternoon! My name is Mrs Moore, and I couldn't help noticing your lovely boat,' she said.

Captain O'Malley frowned a little. 'Although I'm proud of her, I wouldn't describe her as lovely.'

'It's the name I like. I love herrings.'

MURDER IN THE BAY

'Do you now?' The captain took off his cap and scratched his head. 'You sound American.'

'I am! This is my assistant, Miss Sprigg. We're staying at Lady Florence's house.'

He raised his eyebrows. 'Lady Florence?'

'Yes, it's been very upsetting. She invited us to stay with her and then the awful tragedy happened. We're staying on down here just in case we can be of any help to Miss Trent. She's desperately upset about losing her employer and companion. Did you know Lady Florence well?'

He shook his head. 'No, not well at all. But I was sad to hear the news.'

'Yes, we're still trying to recover from the shock. Little walks like this one help us immensely. It's lovely to be by the sea. I live in London and the closest I get to any water is the River Thames.'

'I can't imagine being away from the sea.'

'Have you lived here all your life?'

'I was born here and grew up here. Then I spent thirty years in the Navy. These days I potter about on this boat. Fernwood's my home, but I start to feel a little strange if I spend too much time on land. There's a lot of comfort in bobbing up and down on the water.'

Mrs Moore laughed. 'I can't empathise with that at all, but I think it's wonderful you enjoy it so much. Do you go about everywhere by boat?'

'Oh yes.'

'I hear you have to be careful around here. Shipwreck Point is clearly so-called for a reason.'

'Oh yes, you have to know what you're doing. If you're an inexperienced sailor, then I don't advise sailing near that headland. But I know the rocks there like the back of my hand. They don't pose a problem to me.'

'And do you always go about in this boat, or do you have a smaller boat as well?'

'Only my rowing boat.'

'Oh lovely. Do you use it often?'

'Often enough.'

'How lovely. Your life isn't one I can imagine for myself. I enjoy being by the sea and looking at it. But I don't particularly enjoy being on it. I think it's best left to the sea creatures.'

He chuckled. 'Perhaps you could come on a boat trip with me, Mrs Moore?'

'My sea legs aren't very good.'

'Perhaps you've not been on the right sort of boat, Mrs Moore. I'm always encouraging landlubbers to get out onto the sea. There's something quite humbling about being out there. The feeling of being so small between the sea and the sky. You become part of it, somehow.'

'Goodness, Captain O'Malley. That sounds quite poetic.'

He nodded. 'Some people think I'm little more than an old rum-swilling seadog. But I'm quite the sensitive type, you know.' He gave a wink.

Mrs Moore chuckled. 'Are you really, Captain O'Malley?'

'Come on a boat trip with me and you'll find out. And please bring Miss Sprigg and the dog, too. Does the dog like being on the water?'

'The dog is Rosie. She's from Venice, so she's quite accustomed to water.'

'Perfect! How about tomorrow?'

'Very well, Captain O'Malley. You've persuaded me. We'll see you then.'

Chapter Thirty-One

LOTTIE, Rosie and Mrs Moore returned to Tidecrest House. They'd just joined Miss Trent in the sitting room when the butler informed her Lord Cavendish had arrived.

'Oh dear, really? I suppose you had better show him in then.'

Lord Cavendish wore a black mourning suit. He looked weary and his handlebar moustache drooped at the ends.

'How are you bearing up, Lord Cavendish?' asked Mrs Moore.

He pulled his pipe from his mouth to reply. 'I've been better. It's rather difficult being in this house. I feel like Florence is still here.'

'Yes, it does feel like she's still here,' said Miss Trent. 'In fact, I believe she is. In spirit.'

Lord Cavendish gave a shiver. 'No, don't talk about spirits, Marianne. I don't like the idea of being haunted.'

'What have you come to see us about, Lord Cavendish?' asked Miss Trent.

'I'd like to have a little look about, if you don't mind.

97

There are a few things of mine lying around which I would like to take back.'

He strolled over to a mahogany display cabinet. 'This Royal Vienna vase, for example. It belonged to my father. I don't think it's worth much, but it has sentimental value. But I wouldn't mind taking that back if that's alright. The crystal cut-glass decanter was my mother's.'

'I thought you took all your belongings at the time of the divorce,' said Miss Trent.

'Yes, most of my things. But I had to leave some here because I was going off to America. I couldn't risk them being knocked about and getting broken. You wouldn't believe the way they chuck tea chests around on transatlantic ships. I agreed with Florence that I would leave them here for safe-keeping.'

'I don't recall that,' said Miss Trent. 'I think Lady Florence would have told me about it.'

'Florence didn't tell you everything, Marianne.'

'Yes, she did. And I was always under the impression that everything left here was solely Lady Florence's.'

'And most of it is. I mean, look what she got out of me! Pretty much everything. We just agreed I would leave a few sentimental items with her for safekeeping.'

'Did you make a list of them?' asked Miss Trent.

'A list? No, we didn't need a list. There were only a few things.'

'What else did you leave here for safekeeping?'

'There's the grandfather clock in the entrance hall. And there's some silverware in the dining room. The clock on the mantlepiece in the drawing room belonged to my mother. I'll have to have a look around the house to remind myself of the other things.'

'That's quite a long list of things.'

'Yes, but it still isn't much. You've still got everything else.

And you're welcome to the paintings, they're only of old family members who are best forgotten about.'

Miss Trent got to her feet. 'Perhaps you can write down a list of all the items you supposedly left here for safekeeping, Lord Cavendish. Then I can have a look at it?'

'*Supposedly* left here for safekeeping? We agreed it! Now look here, Marianne. We're both as upset as each other about Florence's passing. But making life difficult for each other now won't help matters. It won't make you feel any better, you know.'

'I'm not being difficult and I'm not saying this to make myself feel better!' said Miss Trent, growing tearful. 'But all these things you mention are in the inventory in Lady Florence's will. She never once mentioned to me she was looking after them for you to take away one day.'

'That was her solicitor's mistake,' said Lord Cavendish. 'They shouldn't have been listed in the inventory in the will. And besides, haven't you got enough? You've got this entire house and just about everything in it. And the land and the beach. Surely it's not too much for me to ask for a few items which belonged to my parents? If you're going to be difficult about this, then I will have to engage the services of a lawyer.'

'Oh no, there's no need for that!'

'Right. Then I'll give you a few days to think about it.' He patted his pockets. 'Now, do I have a... oh, this will do.' He pulled out a diary with a little pen attached. He scribbled something down inside it, then he ripped out the page. 'Here,' he held out the piece of paper. 'This is the number of the hotel I'm staying at and my room number. Let me know whether or not I need to get my lawyer involved.'

Miss Trent took the piece of paper from him. 'Very well.'

'Now my pipe's gone out.' He put the diary on the coffee table while he relit his pipe.

Once he was done, he bid them farewell.

. . .

'Quite astonishing!' said Mrs Moore after Lord Cavendish had left. 'The man just wanted to help himself, didn't he?'

'Yes, he did.' Miss Trent sat down. She seemed quite shaken by the conversation. 'I hope I said the right thing. I couldn't allow him to come in and take whatever he wanted. Lady Florence wouldn't have liked that.'

'You're absolutely right, Marianne, she wouldn't have. You did well to stand your ground. He's not an easy person to stand up to.'

'He claims the items he mentions have sentimental value to him,' said Miss Trent. 'But I feel sure that he's just coming up with reasons to help himself to whatever he wants. I can't bear the thought of a lawyer being involved!'

'It's probably just an empty threat,' said Mrs Moore.

'But what if it isn't? It's already difficult enough with the police.'

'The police? Why?'

'Detective Lynton spoke to me again today, and I think I'm in big trouble. No matter how much I explain I was tidying the study when Lady Florence died, he doesn't believe me!'

'Oh dear.'

'It's warm in here, isn't it? I need to get outside and get some air.'

'I'll come with you, Marianne,' said Mrs Moore. 'We need to make sure you're alright.'

Chapter Thirty-Two

LOTTIE GOT up to fetch a book from her room when she noticed something lying on the coffee table.

Lord Cavendish's diary.

'He's left it behind!' she whispered to Rosie.

Lottie reasoned it wouldn't be long before Lord Cavendish noticed it was missing. She picked up the diary and flipped through the pages. The entries weren't easy to read, the handwriting was small and cramped. Lottie turned to the day of Lady Florence's death, but nothing was written there. She flicked back a few weeks and there were some indecipherable appointments and a note about a ship. Presumably it had been the ship Lord Cavendish had travelled on when he arrived back from America.

Lottie turned to the week ahead and saw an appointment on Thursday evening: "Black Anchor, 7".

Then she heard voices beyond the sitting room door. She dropped the diary onto the coffee table and flung herself back into her chair just as the door opened and the butler entered with Lord Cavendish.

'There it is!' said Lord Cavendish, picking up the diary. 'Just where I left it.' He put it in his pocket, bid farewell to Lottie again, and left the room with the butler.

'Black Anchor,' Lottie whispered to Rosie. 'What's that?'

Chapter Thirty-Three

As Lottie walked to her room to fetch her book, she passed Tilly, the maid.

'Excuse me,' said Lottie. 'Do you know what Black Anchor is?'

Tilly smiled. 'The Black Anchor is an inn in Smuggler's Cove.'

'Smuggler's Cove?'

'It's the local name for Prince's Bay. It's on the other side of Shipwreck Point.'

'Are there still smugglers around here?'

'I don't know,' Tilly shrugged. 'But in the olden days, they used the cove for smuggling. The rocks around there are dangerous, so only skilled sailors take their boats into the cove. And there's a little cave which you can get to by boat at low tide. Apparently, the smugglers used to hide all their contraband in there. Rumour has it there's a tunnel from the cave to the basement of The Black Anchor. It's said they used to carry their contraband through there to the pub. That's what I've heard, but it's probably just an old story.'

'It's a fascinating story,' said Lottie. 'Thank you, Tilly.'

. . .

Later that evening, Lottie knocked on Mrs Moore's door after they had retired for the night. She told Mrs Moore about Lord Cavendish's appointment while her employer sat at her dressing table brushing her hair.

'That was quick thinking of you, Lottie, to have a look in his diary. I'm impressed you managed to find something of interest.'

'But I don't know if it's useful.'

'That depends on who he's meeting, doesn't it? It would be fascinating to know. Why's he going to the trouble of meeting them at an old smuggler's inn when there are plenty of cafes, pubs and restaurants in Fernwood-on-Sea?'

'Perhaps he doesn't want to be seen.'

'Yes, I think that could be likely.'

'I'll need to spy on him.'

'Oh no, Lottie, that's much too risky! He'll see you.'

'No, he won't. I'll hide outside the inn and see who turns up.'

'How do you know there'll be somewhere suitable to hide?'

'We can visit beforehand.'

'When is his appointment? Thursday? That's the day after tomorrow. We have our boat trip with Captain O'Malley tomorrow, so perhaps we can venture down to Smuggler's Cove during the day on Thursday. If we ask Miss Trent's permission, Langley might drive us down there. It sounds like a charming little place.'

'Apparently there's a cave there which smugglers hid their contraband in.'

'I can't wait to see it!'

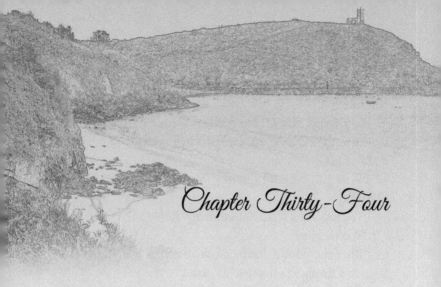

Chapter Thirty-Four

'YOU TURNED UP!' said Captain O'Malley from the bow of his boat when Lottie, Rosie and Mrs Moore arrived at the harbour the following morning.

'Yes,' said Mrs Moore. 'Why wouldn't we?'

'Not everyone turns up when they say they will.' He lowered a rickety-looking gangplank for them.

'The last time I went on a boat, there was a storm,' said Mrs Moore as the captain helped her aboard. Lottie and Rosie followed.

'You don't need to be worrying about any storms today, Mrs Moore. The sea's as calm as a millpond today. Where-abouts were you sailing?'

'Just off the coast of Monaco. I was a guest on Prince Manfred of Bavaria's boat.'

Captain O'Malley raised his bushy eyebrows. 'A Prince in Monaco? I didn't realise you kept such company, Mrs Moore.'

'He wasn't as grand as I thought he was. But it was fun while it lasted.'

The captain cackled. 'Isn't that often the way?'

He started the engine, unhooked the boat's ropes from the

quayside and brought up the gangplank. Then he positioned himself at the wheel and manoeuvred the boat out of the harbour.

Lottie and Mrs Moore perched themselves on a wooden bench in the cabin. Rosie looked a little perturbed, so Lottie cuddled her on her lap.

'Were you born into money, Mrs Moore?' asked Captain O'Malley.

'Yes, my father was a railroad magnate.'

'Was he now?'

'But I should add that he made his own way in life. He was born in a shepherd's bothy in Scotland.'

'Was he indeed? I always admire a man who's pulled himself up by his bootstraps. That's the spirit. I can imagine his daughter has the same approach to life.'

'Oh, I don't know about that, Captain O'Malley.' Mrs Moore giggled. 'I just enjoy travelling and meeting people. That's all there is to it. I don't think I've got any greater calling than that. Oh look, we're already passing the beach at Tidecrest House.'

'We are indeed. Fancy having a look through the telescope?'

'Oh, go on then.'

He passed a telescope to Mrs Moore as they chugged past the golden stretch of sand. The house sat prominently on the slope above it.

Mrs Moore made her way to the stern of the boat and pulled a grimace as she attempted to focus the telescope. 'They can be a fiddle these things, can't they? Especially when you're on a boat moving up and down. Oh, I think I've got something now. Oh... erm... I see.'

'What is it?' said Lottie.

'The garden.' Mrs Moore grimaced again and passed the telescope to Lottie.

It took a moment to train the telescope on the right place, but Lottie managed to find Tidecrest House and then moved the telescope down a little to the sloping lawn. She could see two figures sitting close together on a rug.

'Is that Miss Trent?' she said.

'I think so.'

'She's laughing with someone,' said Lottie. 'And it looks like... oh. Dr Blackwood?'

'That's who it looks like to me,' said Mrs Moore. 'They appear to know each other quite well. She gave us no indication of that, did she?'

'No,' said Lottie.

Mrs Moore and Lottie returned to the boat's cabin.

'Supposing we wanted to moor at what was Lady Florence's beach,' said Mrs Moore. 'Would that be possible in this boat?'

'No, the water's too shallow there,' said Captain O'Malley. 'It gets deep quickly, that's where the slipway from the boathouse is. But still not deep enough for this boat.'

'So you would put down anchor somewhere and then get into a rowing boat and row up to the beach?'

'Yes, that's how you do it, Mrs Moore.'

The boat moved on and the garden of Tidecrest House receded into the distance. They were nearing Shipwreck Point now, and Lottie looked up at the little church she'd visited the previous day.

Despite the calm waves, there was still white water where they crashed onto the rocks at the foot of the cliff.

'Those rocks look dastardly,' said Mrs Moore.

'They are,' said the captain. 'Many a good ship's been lost around here. Luckily, you're safe with me. Although I once had a knotty moment on a foggy day out here. That's when I saw the ghost ship.'

'Oh no, please don't tell me ghost stories, Captain O'Malley. I don't believe in them.'

'But when you see a ghost ship, you see it. It doesn't matter whether you believe in it or not.'

'What exactly did you see?' asked Mrs Moore.

Captain O'Malley turned off the boat's engine so all was quiet. The boat bobbed gently on the waves just by the headland of Shipwreck Point.

'You want to know what I saw, Mrs Moore?'

'Yes.'

'You're not going to scoff at it?'

'No. I'm not going to scoff at all.'

'Are you going to scoff?' he asked Lottie.

'No,' said Lottie. 'I never scoff.'

'Good. Because I know what I saw. You wouldn't have believed the fog and mist on that day. A terrible sea fret, it was. Came in from nowhere. The worst I've ever seen! And although I know this place like the back of my hand, even the most familiar place is unfamiliar when the fog comes in.'

'I know exactly what you mean,' said Mrs Moore. 'When we get those terrible fogs in London, I barely recognise my own street.'

'Well, there you go, Mrs Moore. You know what it's like. The fog came in and I struggled to find my bearings. With no proper sight of the horizon or the sun in the sky, I was completely disorientated!

'I knew I'd have to sit it out until the fret lifted. But I was worried my boat would be carried onto the rocks. And in that thick mist, I had no idea where the rocks were! And then... I saw it.'

His voice grew quiet, and Lottie felt a shiver run down her back.

'The ghost ship?' said Mrs Moore.

'It looked like an old galleon. The sort they had a few hundred years ago. I've never seen a boat as old as that before or since. It just loomed up on my starboard side. As silent as the moon's glow.'

'Goodness.'

'And do you know what?'

'What?'

'There wasn't a soul on it.'

'No one on it?'

'No one. And I'll tell you something else strange.'

'What?'

'It was in full sail and was moving by an unseen wind.'

'How spooky.'

'It was no wind I could feel at that time. I watched as it drew closer to me and I realised that if I didn't change course, then I was going to collide with it!'

'But if it was an apparition, surely you'd have just passed through it?'

'It didn't look like an apparition to me, Mrs Moore. It looked as solid as you are now sitting on that seat.'

'Really? Golly.'

'I shouted out to the ship and sounded my boat's horn. It was in my way! But there was no response at all. It just sailed on, silently. Crossing my path. I wasn't too happy about it, but I had to alter my course. Quite drastically, too.'

'Goodness. Then what?'

'It disappeared into the mist. And as soon as it had done so, the fret began to lift. Within ten minutes there was no sign of the sea fret at all!'

'Goodness. Any sign of the galleon?'

'None.'

'How strange.'

'And that was when I realised I was closer to the headland than I'd thought. And when I looked closer, I noticed the galleon had been right where the rocks are! By rights it should have run aground on them!'

'But it didn't.'

'No! And if that ship hadn't forced me to change my course, then I would have ended up on those rocks myself!'

'Goodness me,' said Mrs Moore. 'So the ghost ship saved your life?'

'I believe it did. So the next time you say you don't believe in ghosts, Mrs Moore, just stop and have a think about it. Because you can never be completely sure. I like to think the sea was looking after me that day, after all my decades of service.'

Chapter Thirty-Five

CAPTAIN O'MALLEY STARTED the boat's engine.

'Is Smuggler's Cove near here?' Mrs Moore asked him.

'How has an outsider like you heard of that place?'

'Someone mentioned it the other day. One of Lady Florence's servants, I think.'

'It's just on the other side of the headland.'

'Can we visit it?'

'Not in this boat.'

'And does the cove have a smuggling history?'

'That's what they say. I don't like the look of those clouds over there, I think we should head back.'

'Which clouds?'

'On the horizon over there.'

Lottie squinted and could just make out a little bit of grey where the sea met the sky.

'It may look like nothing,' said the captain. 'But you'd be surprised how quickly a weather system can move in.'

'Well, you're the expert, so we'll take your word for it,' said Mrs Moore.

As Captain O'Malley turned the boat around, Mrs Moore

spoke into Lottie's ear. 'His mood has changed hasn't it, Lottie? Do you think it was something I said?'

'Maybe it was when you mentioned the cove.'

'Interesting. Shall I ask him about the rowing boat on Lady Florence's beach? I feel we don't have much time left with him.'

'It's worth a try.'

Mrs Moore cleared her throat and spoke up. 'Have you heard about the rowing boat which was seen on Lady Florence's beach at the time of her murder, Captain O'Malley?'

'No. Not heard about that.'

'Do you know many people with a rowing boat?'

'Lots of people. I've got one myself.'

'Oh yes, I suppose you have. I don't suppose it could have been your boat, could it?'

He turned to her and scowled. 'Why would it have been my boat?'

'I don't know. The detective is trying to find out who it belonged to.'

'Wasn't mine. Must have been someone else's.' He turned back to his wheel and steered the boat towards the harbour. They passed the beach of Tidecrest House again, and Lottie wondered if Miss Trent was still entertaining Dr Blackwood.

'Have you got any idea who else the detective could ask about the rowing boat?'

'Like I've said, lots of people own rowing boats.'

'Yes, I understand. And they all look quite similar, I suppose.'

'They do.'

'If the police could find the owner of the rowing boat seen on the beach that evening, then they'll be able to find out who was close by when Lady Florence was murdered.'

'Or find the murderer. That's what you really mean, isn't it, Mrs Moore?'

'Well... maybe. It's a possibility, isn't it? The murderer could have got to Lady Florence's beach in a rowing boat.'

'Perhaps he did. But I'll tell you now, Mrs Moore. It wasn't me.'

'Oh, I certainly wasn't accusing you of anything, Captain O'Malley! I was just wondering if you could help the police find the owner of that boat. But never mind.'

'I didn't know Lady Florence well,' said the captain. 'But I'll tell you something I noticed. Lord Cavendish returned from a few years in America and, days later, his former wife is dead.'

'You think Lord Cavendish could have done it?' asked Mrs Moore.

'I'm not one for pointing the finger. But it seems like more than a coincidence to me. It didn't work out for Lord Cavendish in America so he came back here hoping to move into his house again. I didn't know Lady Florence well, but I can't imagine her being pleased about it. After the divorce, she was probably happy to see the back of him and thought she could live the rest of her years here in peace. But then he came back. It would have ruffled her feathers, I feel sure of it.'

'It would have caused a dispute between them?'

'A big dispute! She wouldn't have wanted him here, that's for sure. And perhaps he decided to take matters into his own hands.'

'Murder?'

'Who knows? I'm not saying it's impossible.'

Chapter Thirty-Six

AFTER THE BOAT TRIP, Lottie and Mrs Moore visited the tea shop on the harbour front. It was the same tea shop Mrs Moore had shown an interest in on their walk to Windy Edge with Lady Florence.

They sat at an outside table with a gingham tablecloth. The striped awning overhead gave them some shade.

Rosie rested beneath the table. She seemed relieved to be off the boat.

'Well, the boat trip was quite fun, wasn't it, Lottie? Although I can't say we got a great deal of information from Captain O'Malley. He was adamant that it wasn't his rowing boat which was seen on the beach.'

'And perhaps it wasn't,' said Lottie. 'But I'm not sure whether to believe him. He claimed not to know Lady Florence, but he had opinions on how she would have felt about Lord Cavendish returning.'

'Yes, I thought that was interesting. I got the impression he knew her a little better than he was letting on. Until the police can confirm who the rowing boat belonged to, then he's probably a suspect. Although I have no idea what his motive would have been.'

A waitress arrived with their afternoon tea. There were freshly baked scones, pots of jam and cream, and an enormous teapot. A seagull rested on a signpost close by, eyeing them.

'Watch out for him,' said Mrs Moore, peering at the gull through her lorgnette. 'He'll be after our food given half the chance.'

'What do you make of Miss Trent and Dr Blackwood in the garden together?' asked Lottie.

'Quite astonishing!' Mrs Moore paused from stirring the tea. 'Marianne didn't mention Dr Blackwood was planning to visit, did she?'

'Unless he turned up with no notice again.'

'Even if he did, they looked quite close on that lawn together. And they appeared to be sharing a joke. It was surprising to see them laughing in the wake of Lady Florence's tragic death. We'll have to ask Marianne about him when we get back to the house.'

'I've got a better idea,' said Lottie. 'Let's not mention him at all. She might feel uncomfortable learning that we peered at her through a telescope from Captain O'Malley's boat. Let's see if she tells us Dr Blackwood visited. If she doesn't mention his visit at all, then it's a sign she's hiding something.'

'What a good idea, Lottie. She's definitely hiding something, isn't she? It sounds like the detective is on to her, too. But if she did murder Lady Florence, then how do we explain Captain O'Malley's rowing boat on the beach?'

'It might not be his.'

'Of course. I wish we knew who it belonged to.'

'We still only have Dr Blackwood's word it was there.'

'True!'

'Miss Trent is unaccounted for at the time of Lady

Florence's death,' said Lottie. 'And Dr Blackwood could have lied about the rowing boat.'

'So he knows she did it?'

'They could have been in on it together.'

Mrs Moore's jaw dropped. 'By golly, they could have been! Perhaps Miss Trent is going to share her fortune with him!'

Chapter Thirty-Seven

THE SEAGULL HOPPED down from its signpost, trying to get a closer look at the scones. But Rosie spotted it and chased it away.

'I say,' said a lady at the table next to them. 'Isn't your dog good at keeping the gulls away? The tea shop should employ it.'

'There's a thought,' said Mrs Moore.

'A lovely dog. A corgi, isn't it? What's its name?'

'Rosie,' said Lottie.

'I'd like to have another dog one day. My dog died three years ago, and I'm still not over it.'

'I'm sorry to hear it,' said Mrs Moore.

'You're not from around here, are you?' said the lady. She had grey wavy hair and steel-rimmed spectacles. She wore a lemon-yellow summer dress.

'No,' said Mrs Moore. 'I'm not from these parts. I'm an American who lives in London. But I like to travel about, and we came down here to stay with a friend.'

The lady's eyes narrowed. 'Which friend?'

'Lady Florence.'

Her eyes pinged wide open, and she shuffled her chair closer. 'Oh goodness. What a time to come down here and stay with her. What's it been like at Tidecrest House?'

'It's not been easy. We're keeping Miss Trent company while the police investigate the matter.'

'I expect you are.' Without asking, the woman pulled her chair over to their table and joined them. 'How's Miss Trent keeping?'

'She's very upset.' Lottie thought of her laughing on the lawn with Dr Blackwood. 'But she's managing as well as she can,' added Mrs Moore.

'I've heard she's got it all now. The house and everything.'

'Yes. Lady Florence left it to her.'

'Unimaginable. I wouldn't know where to start if I were left an estate like that. It must be a nice problem to have.'

'Yes. She's lived at the house for many years, so she's quite used to the place.'

'I suppose so. And they say Lord Cavendish returned hoping to get the house back again. I can't see how he's going to manage that. I'm Geraldine Collins, by the way. Mrs.'

'Nice to meet you, Mrs Collins. I'm Mrs Moore and this is Miss Sprigg. Did you know Lady Florence at all?'

'A little. I'm afraid to say she wasn't terribly popular around here.'

'So I've heard.'

'She wasn't nasty as such, but she could be quite unkind. I liked her, myself. I don't think she meant to be unkind, she would say things without realising how they sounded. And the trouble is, people are so easily offended these days. Lady Florence came from a time where you could speak your mind and people accepted it. It seems that people's feelings are so easily wounded now.'

'Can you think of anyone who would have wanted to harm her?'

'No. It must have been an outsider. I don't believe anyone living in the village would do something like that.'

'An outsider?'

'Yes. Someone from her past, maybe. An old acquaintance seeking revenge. Or maybe someone wanted to silence her.'

'And what makes you say that?'

Mrs Collins glanced about and lowered her voice. 'There was word that Lady Florence had a past. Few people know where she came from. She arrived in the village thirty years ago. But no one seems to know what she was doing for twenty-five years before then.'

'Were you living here when she arrived?'

'Oh yes. I've lived here all my life and I'm seventy-two now. I remember the day she turned up here. Some said she'd come down from London, while others said she'd been living abroad. Whatever the truth was, she was a lady of independent means. Family money, I expect. Her maiden name was Davis. I know nothing about the Davis family. She rented a cottage on the edge of the village and while she was there, she learned how to sail. She took lessons from someone at the sailing club. And then she vanished.'

'Vanished?'

'Yes. I don't know where. The cottage was rented out to someone else, and no one knew where she had gone. The next thing we knew, she'd married a Lord in London and the pair of them bought old Mrs Harmsworth's house. When old Mrs Harmsworth died, everyone had their eye on that house. The Fitzroy family in particular. They were very keen to buy it. But it was sold quickly to Lord and Lady Cavendish. I don't know how they bought it so fast. The Fitzroys were not happy! But there you have it.'

'So no one knew much about her when she was a younger woman?'

'Lord Cavendish would know, I suppose. We once had a travelling salesman come through here who claimed to have known the Davis family in Surrey. He got talking in one of the pubs one evening and told a wild story about an illegitimate child.'

'Whose illegitimate child?'

'Lady Florence's.'

'Lady Florence had an illegitimate child?'

The lady shrugged. 'I don't know. It was a rumour for a while, but only because the salesman mentioned it in a pub one evening. I never met him. But it makes you wonder, doesn't it? If his story was true, then perhaps Lady Florence's past caught up with her?'

'This is why you have a theory about an outsider committing the crime?'

'Yes.'

'But surely an outsider would have been spotted?'

'Maybe so.'

'And Miss Sprigg and I were staying at the house. We didn't notice any unusual visitors.'

'I can only tell you what I heard, Mrs Moore. If Lady Florence did have an illegitimate child, then it would have been many years ago. Before her marriage to Lord Cavendish. Perhaps she had an argument with someone who knew her secret?'

'There's an interesting thought.'

'Maybe Lord Cavendish found out about it. Or maybe he didn't. We just don't know, do we? But I think the answer to her murder lies in her past.'

'Do you know the reason Lord and Lady Cavendish divorced?' asked Mrs Moore.

'No. But he took himself off to America quite quickly

afterwards. I always wondered if he was running away from something.'

'Such as what?'

'All we can do is guess. You could try asking him yourself, Mrs Moore.'

'I don't think he'd take kindly to that. But it's not a bad idea.'

Chapter Thirty-Eight

'DID you enjoy your boat trip with Captain O'Malley?' Miss Trent asked Lottie and Mrs Moore at dinner that evening.

'Yes, it was very pleasant,' said Mrs Moore. 'Perhaps you caught sight of our boat while we were out there, Marianne?'

'No, I've been much too busy to admire the view today. Lord Cavendish has now provided me with a list of things which he claims are his, so I've been sorting through everything trying to find them.'

'But by rights, everything is yours, Marianne.'

'I suppose so. But having looked at the list, I don't see why I should kick up a fuss about it. The poor chap seems very bereft, and they're not things which I'm going to miss. So it makes sense just to let him have them.'

'That's very gracious of you, Marianne.'

'It just seems easier this way. I can't bear confrontation.' She dipped her spoon into her soup.

'Lottie and I had a conversation with Geraldine Collins at the tea shop by the harbour,' said Mrs Moore. 'Do you know her?'

Miss Trent groaned. 'That woman is a dreadful gossip. I

expect she's got many theories about what happened to Lady Florence.'

'Yes, she did mention some.'

'And what did she have to say for herself? Not that I'm particularly interested. But as it's regarding Lady Florence, I think it's important for me to hear.'

'Mrs Collins's theory is that someone from Lady Florence's past came back and harmed her.'

'Such as who?'

'She didn't mention anyone in particular.'

'That's because she's just speculating.'

'She mentioned a rumour which was apparently started by a travelling salesman.'

Miss Trent groaned again. 'The illegitimate child? It was the talk of the village for a while. I don't know anyone who actually met the travelling salesman, the rumour may have come from someone else. But I asked Lady Florence about it and she assured me there was no truth in it whatsoever.'

'So it was just gossip that Mrs Collins feels the need to mention again.'

'Yes. I pity people like Mrs Collins. Their lives must be so boring that all they can do is talk about other people. And I wouldn't mind so much if they didn't cause harm. But when people spread rumours, there's always someone who believes them. Anyway, I mustn't allow myself to get annoyed by that woman. There's already enough to worry about. It looks like I'm going to be arrested for murder.'

'No!'

'I have no alibi.' She shrugged. 'What can I do?'

'The detective needs evidence before he can charge you with anything.'

'He'll probably make something up. They do that sometimes.'

'Not Detective Lynton, surely?'

'It depends on how desperate he is. If he doesn't arrest the murderer soon, then I'm sure it will be me he goes for instead. I shouldn't really ask this of you, Mrs Moore, but...'

'What?'

'I don't suppose you and Miss Sprigg could say you saw me?'

'When?'

'When I was tidying the study. Perhaps one of you walked past the door and saw me in there tidying. Or maybe I popped into the sitting room briefly to return some books to the shelves. In fact, I'm quite sure I did that.'

'I don't recall you doing it, Marianne.'

'But do you recall me not doing it?'

'Now I'm confused.'

'Exactly! It's all so terribly confusing, isn't it? When we're going about our day-to-day business, we can't remember the exact times we saw people. Perhaps you saw me at a quarter past seven. Or maybe half past? You really can't remember if you did or didn't. But you had a general sense that I was about, didn't you? You know for sure that I hadn't dashed down to the boathouse, murdered poor dear Lady Florence, then dashed back again. You would have known about it if I had.'

'I remember you dashing off to make a telephone call at seven, Marianne,' said Mrs Moore. 'And that's what I told Detective Lynton. I can't say with any certainty that I caught sight of you again before eight.'

Miss Trent's lower lip wobbled. Then she turned to Lottie. 'Miss Sprigg? What do you remember?'

Lottie didn't want to upset her. But she knew she couldn't lie to protect her. She felt sure Miss Trent was up to something. She hadn't admitted Dr Blackwood had visited her, and now she was trying to establish a false alibi.

'I saw you leave the dining room at seven that evening,' she said. 'And then you came into the sitting room just after eight.'

Miss Trent stared at her, as if expecting more.

'That's what I told Detective Lynton,' Lottie added, feeling distinctly uncomfortable. 'I didn't see you between seven and eight, Miss Trent.'

A lengthy pause followed. Miss Trent then sighed and her shoulders slumped. 'Thank you both. I'm sorry. I shouldn't have asked you that. It was wrong of me. I suppose I'm just rather desperate to get out of this pickle I'm in.'

Chapter Thirty-Nine

LANGLEY THE CHAUFFEUR agreed to drive Lottie, Rosie and Mrs Moore to Smuggler's Cove the following day. The road took them over the headland of Shipwreck Point before descending sharply on the other side.

The driver then took a road to the right which was a steep bumpy track with tufts of grass growing in the centre.

'Oh dear,' said Mrs Moore as the motor car struggled down the track. 'Will this damage your vehicle?'

'No madam, it's quite accustomed to rural roads.'

'Oh good. That's a relief then.'

The track zig-zagged down the steep hillside before ending abruptly in a sheltered, rocky cove.

To their left, The Black Anchor inn leant against the cliff face. It was constructed of the same grey granite and looked like it had been there since the beginning of time. It had little mullioned windows and a black anchor was painted on the weatherworn sign.

'There's no beach here,' said Langley. 'Just rocks.'

'So we gathered. We'd like to get out and have a little look around, if that's alright?'

'Of course. You'll find a path on the right. It leads part of the way around the cove, but it's quite steep.'

They thanked him and climbed out of the car. The sky was overcast and as grey as the cliffs. Waves sloshed and spilled on the rocky shore.

'It's quite a bit cooler today, isn't it?' said Mrs Moore. 'Let's have a quick stroll along the path. I don't see how you're going to be able to spy on Lord Cavendish here, Lottie. It's tricky to get to, and where would you hide?'

'Behind a rock.'

'Really? I don't think it's a good idea.'

They followed the path around the cove. It was narrow and covered in shingle. They walked carefully, and Lottie kept Rosie on a short lead.

'I think that must be the cave over there,' said Lottie, pointing to a small opening at the bottom of the cliffs on the opposite side of the cove.

'It must be!' said Mrs Moore. 'And it's linked to the inn by a tunnel?'

'I don't know if that's true or not.'

'I can see why this place would have appealed to smugglers. It's quiet, secluded and not very welcoming.' As she spoke, her foot slipped on the shingle. 'Oh good grief, Lottie. I nearly ended up on the rocks then!'

'I wonder if you still get smugglers here,' said Lottie. 'This cove looks like it hasn't changed in hundreds of years.'

'You're right, Lottie. It could belong to the eighteenth century or whenever it was when pirates still sailed about.'

They paused on the path and surveyed the scene.

'Marianne didn't breathe a word of Dr Blackwood's visit yesterday, did she?' said Mrs Moore. 'And then she tried to persuade us we'd seen her between seven and eight that evening.' She shook her head. 'I wish I knew what she's up to. I want to be kind towards her, but if she's behind

Lady Florence's murder then I want nothing to do with her!'

'I agree,' said Lottie. 'It feels strange being guests under her roof when we don't know whether or not to trust her.'

'Have you been locking your bedroom door at night, Lottie?'

'Yes.'

'Me too. It sounds awful, doesn't it? I just want to find out one way or the other if she committed the crime.'

Lottie spotted movement on the other side of the cove. 'Look!' she said. 'There's someone at the mouth of the cave!'

'What?' Mrs Moore peered through her lorgnette. 'Goodness me, Lottie. There is!'

Lottie squinted. The figure had a beard and appeared to be wearing a fisherman's smock. 'It looks like Captain O'Malley!'

'I think it is! But what on earth can he be doing there?'

They watched as he clambered down the rocks to where a little rowing boat was moored.

'Duck down, Lottie,' said Mrs Moore. 'We don't want him to see us, do we?'

They watched as he stepped into the rowing boat. He untied it, then skilfully navigated the heaving waves as he steered himself out of the cove and out into the sea.

'He didn't want to talk about the cove yesterday, did he, Lottie? And now we know why. He's clearly up to something.'

'Smuggling?'

'It could be. But smuggling what? Oh, this path is too steep now. Let's head back to the car.'

Langley had somehow manoeuvred the motor car at the end of the track so it was facing uphill, ready for their drive back.

They climbed into the car and Mrs Moore thanked

Langley for waiting. 'What's the inn like?' she asked him as he edged the car up the steep track.

'It's a local inn.'

'I see. Few outsiders then?'

'No. They don't really know about it.'

'Well, it's a very quaint little place. Who runs it?'

'Old Mr Saunders. His family have owned it for the past three hundred years.'

'Goodness. And is it true what they say about a secret tunnel between the inn and the cave?'

'It's probably little more than an old story, Mrs Moore. That's the trouble in these parts. The people round here love telling old stories.'

Chapter Forty

'I CAN'T BELIEVE Captain O'Malley would be involved in smuggling,' said Mrs Moore once they were back in her room at Tidecrest House.

'Perhaps the cave is used for another purpose these days,' said Lottie. 'I can't think what for, though.'

'We might have to ask him,' said Mrs Moore.

'Won't he suspect we were spying on him?'

'He might, but we weren't, were we? We went to look at the cove and he happened to be there at the same time.'

'Perhaps Captain O'Malley is the person who Lord Cavendish has arranged to meet at The Black Anchor this evening,' said Lottie.

'Yes, he could be! It's a shame we can't find out for sure.'

'Yes, we can. I'll go there.'

'How?'

'I'll ask Miss Trent if there's a bicycle I can borrow.'

'I'm not sure about this, Lottie.'

'There are plenty of rocks to hide behind in the cove. I can watch the inn and see who turns up at seven o'clock.'

'I don't think it's a good idea.'

'If Lord Cavendish meets with Captain O'Malley, then I think we can be fairly certain it was the captain's rowing boat on the beach that evening.'

'You think the two of them could have arranged to meet that evening, too?'

'It's possible. But we won't know if we don't find out who Lord Cavendish is meeting.'

Mrs Moore sighed. 'Very well. But you must be careful, Lottie. I shall worry about you dreadfully. I'll look after Rosie here.'

'Borrow a bicycle?' said Miss Trent. 'Of course! I think Lady Florence had quite a few. I don't ride them myself. I'll ask Arthur to find a suitable one for you, and he'll make sure it's cleaned up and oiled and the tyres are pumped up. When would you like to borrow it?'

'I'm hoping to go for a bicycle ride this evening.'

'This evening?' Miss Trent pulled a doubtful expression. 'You do realise there's rain forecast for this evening, Miss Sprigg? We've had some lovely evenings, and it's a shame to pick one when the weather's not so good. I think it's going to brighten up again tomorrow.'

'I don't mind a bit of rain,' said Lottie. 'I find it refreshing.'

'Very well.' Miss Trent smiled. 'I'll ask Arthur to sort out a bike for you. What time do you wish to leave?'

'About six.'

'Alright. Actually, I've just had a thought...' Miss Trent tapped her finger on her chin as she considered something. 'Perhaps I could come with you?'

Lottie felt her heart sink. If Miss Trent accompanied her,

Lottie's plan to spy on Lord Cavendish at The Black Anchor would be ruined.

'On second thoughts, I should probably get on with sorting through Lady Florence's papers. The solicitor has given me a list of information he needs. I'll accompany you on a nicer evening, Miss Sprigg.'

* * *

'Here's the bicycle, Miss Sprigg,' said Arthur Harris, wheeling it out of the garage. 'I've replaced the brake pads and tightened up the cables. I've given it a good oiling, but you'll have to watch the saddle because one of the springs needs replacing. It shouldn't cause you too much trouble, although it will probably feel uneven. I've tightened up the handlebars and put some air in the tyres.'

'Thank you, Mr Harris,' said Lottie.

'Watch out for Farmer Tussock on the lanes. You can usually hear his tractor coming before you see him. He likes to drive his tractor as if there's no one else on the road. Be prepared to jump into a hedge if need be.'

'Thank you for the warning,' said Lottie.

She took the bicycle from him, and Arthur surveyed the sky with his hands on his hips.

'Weather doesn't look too good this evening. Mind you don't get wet.'

Lottie thanked Arthur again, climbed onto the bicycle, and pedalled towards the long driveway. It took a few minutes to get accustomed to cycling again. The last time she'd ridden a bicycle had been in Paris.

A cool breeze whipped at her hair as she cycled along the meandering drive. When she reached the lane, she turned right and followed the route Langley had driven earlier that day.

The road rose uphill, and Lottie's legs began to ache as she pedalled up the incline. The road became so steep that Lottie had to dismount and walk the bicycle to the top of the hill. She could now see Shipwreck Point and the silhouette of the church. A dark cloud loomed ominously in the sky beyond it.

At the top of the hill, Lottie clambered back onto the bicycle and enjoyed freewheeling downhill. The road descended and snaked its way through a patch of woodland. The hedgerows rose high on either side, and Lottie heard an engine growing louder.

She braked a little and a red tractor careered around the bend in front of her. There was barely enough time to get out of its way. Lottie had to stop and lean into the hedge. The man driving the tractor gave her a friendly wave as he passed.

Lottie recognised the turn to the right, which led down to Smuggler's Cove. She cycled slowly over the bumps, stones and grass on the track. Eventually, she reached the cove.

All was quiet apart from the crash of waves. There was no sign of activity at The Black Anchor inn. Lottie took the little shingle path she had walked along with Mrs Moore and found a rocky place to shelter with the bicycle. Peering over a rock, she could see the old timber door of the inn. She would be able to see everyone who arrived and left.

Lottie settled down and waited.

The dark cloud was closer now and Lottie felt spots of rain. She hoped she wouldn't have to wait for too long.

After five minutes, she heard the distant throb of an engine. Gradually, the sound grew louder, like an angry buzzing bee.

Someone was coming down the track.

Lottie stayed as still as she could and watched.

A motorcycle came into view. A figure in tweed sat astride it. The motorcycle came to a halt by the inn, and the rider got off and leaned the machine against the inn's wall. The rider wore a cap which covered his ears and fastened beneath his chin. He also wore goggles and thick gloves. He removed his gloves and rested them on the seat of the motorcycle. Then he began to unfasten the strap beneath his chin.

Lottie held her breath.

Chapter Forty-One

THE MOTORCYCLIST PULLED off his hat.

It was Lord Cavendish.

Lottie gave a little gasp of surprise, she hadn't realised he rode a motorcycle.

She watched him push open the heavy inn door and disappear inside.

Now Lottie had to wait for his companion.

The sky darkened, and the raindrops became more frequent. Lottie tucked herself closer to the rocks, trying to shelter. She chastised herself for not bringing a rain jacket with her.

Five minutes passed. Then another five.

No one else arrived at the inn.

The rain fell steadily, and Lottie's cardigan was soon wet through. Gusts of wind blew around the cove and took the rain with it. Soon it was coming at Lottie from a sideways direction, as well as overhead.

She was drenched. And there was no sign of the person Lord Cavendish was meeting. Had they already been in the Black Anchor when she arrived?

Lottie shivered. She was cold now and risked catching a chill if she stayed out in the rain any longer.

She would have to go into the inn.

Lottie wheeled her bicycle along the path back towards The Black Anchor. It had been a mistake coming here. She should have listened to Mrs Moore and decided against it. She should also have heeded Miss Trent's and Arthur's warnings about the weather forecast.

She lay the bicycle on the ground by the inn, reasoning the wind would probably blow it over if she propped it against the wall.

Then she paused at the inn door.

With a bit of luck, there would be a number of people inside, and Lord Cavendish wouldn't notice her. She decided to ask the barman if she could sit in a corner and dry out until the rain passed.

Lottie took in a breath and pushed against the heavy timber door. It swung open, and she stepped into a little bar.

It was silent inside and smelled of beer. The barman paused from polishing a tankard and stared at her.

The bar was small with a low, timbered ceiling. Sawdust covered the floor and there were three old oak tables with stools. Lottie regretted stepping in through the door, there was nowhere to hide.

Apart from the barman, there were only two people present.

Lord Cavendish and Dr Blackwood.

'Good heavens!' said Lord Cavendish. He pulled his pipe out of his mouth and got to his feet. 'Are you alright young miss?' He took a step towards her. 'Just a moment, I recognise you. Miss Sprigg, isn't it?'

Lottie nodded. 'Yes, my lord.'

'Miss Sprigg?' said Dr Blackwood. They both looked concerned.

'Did you fall into the sea?'

'No. It's just the rain.'

'You're soaked to the skin!' said Lord Cavendish. He turned to the barman. 'Light the fire, Simpson. I know it's the middle of summer, but the weather has clearly turned inclement out there.' He took Lottie's arm and guided her to a chair by the fireplace. 'And fetch some blankets and a brandy for this young lady. She needs to warm up.'

Chapter Forty-Two

THERE WAS SOON a roaring fire in the grate, and Lottie felt warmed by the brandy. She huddled under a thick woollen blanket which itched the back of her neck.

'So how on earth did you get here, Miss Sprigg?' asked Lord Cavendish.

'I went out on a bicycle ride,' said Lottie. 'I got lost and I came in here to ask for directions.'

'What an evening to pick for a bicycle ride!' said Dr Blackwood. 'Did you not see the forecast?'

'No.' Lottie decided to act helpless and bewildered.

'Go easy on the young girl, Blackwood,' said Lord Cavendish. 'She's an outsider and unaccustomed to the coastal storms we get here.' He turned back to Lottie. 'You got lost, you say? Where were you heading to?'

'I was looking for Smuggler's Cove,' she said.

'But you're in it,' he chuckled.

'Am I? Perhaps I got confused then. I heard there was a beach in the cove.'

'Who told you that?'

'One of the servants.'

'Perhaps you misheard them, Miss Sprigg. There's no beach here.'

'Well, I'm pleased to learn that I found the place I was looking for. I should have paid more attention to the weather forecast, though.'

'Yes, you should have done, young lady,' said Dr Blackwood.

'The weather must have come in quickly,' said Lord Cavendish. 'It was only spitting with rain when I arrived.'

'Well, if it's bad out there now, you can both travel back in the taxi with me,' said Dr Blackwood. 'He's picking me up in half an hour. You can come back tomorrow to fetch your bicycle and motorcycle.'

'That sounds like a plan, Blackwood,' said Lord Cavendish. 'I don't fancy getting soaked through like Miss Sprigg.'

'It's a surprise to see you both here,' said Lottie.

'Yes, I suppose it must be. I needed to have a chat with Dr Blackwood about a erm... small medical matter. We needed somewhere quiet to talk.'

Dr Blackwood affirmed this with a nod, and Lottie suspected neither man was telling the truth.

* * *

'Dr Blackwood and Lord Cavendish were discussing a medical matter?' said Mrs Moore. 'Why didn't Lord Cavendish visit Dr Blackwood at his surgery like the other patients?'

She had helped Lottie to her bed after she'd returned to Tidecrest House in her damp clothes. Now Lottie sat resting against her pillows with a mug of warm whisky and honey.

'I didn't want to ask them too many questions,' said

Lottie. 'But I suspect they were meeting there for another reason.'

'They must have been. Well at least the mystery is partly solved for now.' She tucked in the bedcovers around Lottie. 'Finish off your hot toddy and get some sleep now.'

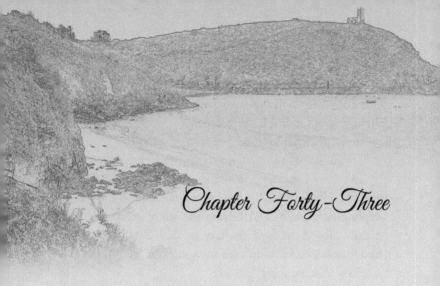

Chapter Forty-Three

MISS TRENT WAS quiet at breakfast the following morning. She muttered to herself while eating her boiled egg and dabbed her eyes with her handkerchief while buttering her toast.

Lottie and Mrs Moore exchanged a concerned glance.

'Are you alright, Marianne?' asked Mrs Moore.

'Yes. I'm fine.' She raised her toast to her mouth to take a bite. But a sob interrupted her and she dropped her toast onto the floor. Duke trotted over and gobbled it up.

'Oh dear, Marianne!' Mrs Moore got up from her seat and went over to her. 'What's wrong?'

'Oh, it's been unbearable. And I've been so terribly stupid!'

'I'm sure you haven't Marianne.' Mrs Moore reached for the teapot and topped up her cup of tea. 'But why don't you tell us all about it?'

Miss Trent sniffed. 'I'm afraid I have a confession to make.'

Lottie held her breath. Was Miss Trent going to admit to murder?

'Being questioned by the police makes you feel you've done something wrong, doesn't it?' said Miss Trent. 'And I've done absolutely nothing wrong! Well, I have, and I'm quite ashamed about it. But it's not actually wrong in the eyes of the law. If you get what I mean.'

'I think so,' said Mrs Moore, returning to her chair.

'Detective Lynton keeps asking me what I was doing at the time of Lady Florence's death. And I made up a story about telephoning an aunt and tidying the study because I didn't have an alibi. Actually, I do have an alibi. But there's a very good reason why I couldn't tell anyone about the alibi.'

'So who is the alibi?'

She gave another sniff. 'Edward Blackwood!'

'Oh?'

'Oh, I've been so foolish! I'm ashamed to admit it, Mrs Moore, but I've been having an affair with him for the past three months. He swore me to secrecy because he's married. Although he has nothing to do with his wife.'

'Of course not.'

'But he also didn't want Lady Florence to find out. We both knew she would have been difficult about it. So we've just been in the habit of keeping it completely secret. Anyway, on the evening Lady Florence died, we had arranged to meet in the woods near the beach.'

'Which is why you dashed off at seven o'clock saying you had to make a telephone call,' said Lottie.

'That's right.'

'And that's why Dr Blackwood was walking along the beach at the time of Lady Florence's murder and saw the rowing boat there.'

'Yes. And I know he saw the rowing boat there because he asked me about it. He asked me who was visiting Lady Florence, and I told her I didn't know. I said she'd gone out for a sail and I don't know why there was a rowing boat on the beach. Anyway, we met up, as we had planned to. And then when I heard what had happened to Lady Florence, I felt so dreadful about it all. I felt bad about having lied to her. Well, I didn't lie to her, I just kept a secret from her. If only I had gone down to the boathouse to check on her, I could have stopped her murderer in his tracks. But instead, I was with Dr Blackwood. We went for a little stroll together and we didn't know that someone was attacking Lady Florence at the time. I feel so awful about it!'

'How could you possibly have known someone was attacking her?' said Mrs Moore. 'You mustn't feel bad about not having checked on her. She planned to go for a sail as she often did. She didn't really need checking up on, she was a grown woman. No one could have predicted that someone would turn up and attack her in that way.'

'No, I suppose not. But I still feel awful about it. And I'll have to tell the detective the truth now so they don't arrest me for not having an alibi. And Edward is going to be so angry with me!'

'He shouldn't be.'

'They're going to ask him about the alibi. And what if his wife finds out?'

'If it's true that he has nothing to do with her, then presumably she won't be particularly bothered.'

'And even when I do tell the detective the truth, I'm worried it looks bad for both Edward and me. It looks like we both murdered Lady Florence!'

'Why does it look like that?'

'Because we were both near the scene of the murder. And we've just got each other for an alibi. It could look like we're covering for each other, couldn't it?'

'Well, if you tell Detective Lynton the truth, then I don't see why he would think that. And besides, why would either of you want to murder Lady Florence?'

'She was a friend to me!'

'I know. I appreciate you for being honest with us, Marianne,' said Mrs Moore. 'I know it can't be easy. And hopefully when you tell the police the truth, they'll be one step closer to finding out what happened to Lady Florence. We sometimes find ourselves in these situations which aren't perfect. But it's important not to feel ashamed and to tell everyone what you know.'

Miss Trent nodded and blew her nose on her handkerchief. 'I realise that now. I really thought my meeting with Edward that evening didn't matter. I thought I could pretend I was pottering about the house and everyone would accept that. But Detective Lynton kept asking me and asking me, and it all became too much.'

'That's what good detectives do,' said Mrs Moore. 'They get the truth from you. It's always better to tell the truth, Marianne. No matter what the situation is. Do you think Dr Blackwood will tell them the truth, too?'

'Yes, I'll tell him he has to. We need to find who did this to Lady Florence.'

'IT WAS interesting to hear Marianne's confession, wasn't it, Lottie?' said Mrs Moore as they strolled along the beach to Fernwood-on-Sea. The sun was shining again after the rain of the previous evening and the air felt cool and fresh.

'I suppose it explains why we saw her laughing with Dr Blackwood in the garden the other day,' said Lottie. 'But we still don't know whether they conspired to murder Lady Florence.'

'Do you really think they could have? After hearing Marianne's tearful confession?'

'I think Dr Blackwood seems even more suspicious now,' said Lottie. 'Why would he have a relationship with both Lady Florence and Miss Trent? There is no similarity between the two women at all.'

'You're right, Lottie.'

'So I'm not sure Dr Blackwood is motivated by love,' said Lottie. 'I think it's more likely to be money.'

'Golly. I hadn't considered that.'

'Dr Blackwood could have been interested in Lady Florence because he wanted to benefit from her fortune,' said

Lottie. 'But when she put an end to their relationship, he turned his attentions to Miss Trent.'

'But how could he have benefitted from Lady Florence's fortune if he was already married?'

'Perhaps he planned to divorce his wife and propose to Lady Florence. Or maybe he was just hoping for a generous gift or two?'

'And do you think he knew Marianne was set to inherit the estate?'

'I think it's possible,' said Lottie. 'Either Lady Florence or Miss Trent could have told him. And do you remember him telling us how much he'd cared about Lady Florence and hadn't recovered from their break-up?'

'Yes. That made me feel quite uncomfortable. And Marianne was there too, listening to it! I wonder what she must have thought.'

'I think he pretended to be upset to cover up the fact he'd only been interested in Lady Florence for her money.'

'Yes. He wants us to think he was genuinely in love with her. But we don't believe him, do we?'

They reached the harbour wall and climbed the steps to the harbour.

'If Dr Blackwood had a relationship with Lady Florence to benefit from her money,' continued Mrs Moore, 'then he would have been disappointed when she ended their affair. And having discovered Marianne would inherit Lady Florence's estate, he could have turned his attention to her to get his hands on some of the money. This theory gives him a motive for murdering Lady Florence, doesn't it? Do you think he could be that ruthless?'

'He could be. And maybe he's planning to divorce his wife and propose marriage to Miss Trent.'

'Which she would probably accept! Goodness, this could

have happened. But just a moment. Dr Blackwood was with Marianne at the time of Lady Florence's murder.'

'Maybe he met her afterwards? Or maybe Marianne is covering for him?'

'So she still might not be telling the truth? Goodness. I really don't know what to think. Oh, look. There's Captain O'Malley on his boat. Let's ask him about the cave in Smuggler's Cove.' She set off along the harbour wall, and Lottie and Rosie followed.

'Good morning, Captain O'Malley!' called Mrs Moore. 'How are you on this fine morning?'

'I'm very well, thank you, Mrs Moore.' He waved down at her from the bow. 'Don't tell me you want to go on another boat trip again.'

She laughed. 'Not right now. But perhaps another time. I fully enjoyed our little jaunt.'

'I'm pleased to hear it.'

'Oh, there's something I meant to ask you, Captain. Miss Sprigg and I were exploring Smuggler's Cove yesterday.'

'Were you?' His eyes narrowed. 'And what made you decide to do that then?'

'Well, we liked the sound of it, to be honest with you. It sounds like it has a very intriguing history and The Black Anchor inn there looks ancient.'

'Sixteenth century.'

'Goodness, that's ancient indeed. While we were looking around the cove, we happened to notice you there.'

'Me?'

'Yes. We saw you coming out of a little cave. And then you got into your rowing boat and rowed off.'

He gave a laugh. 'That wasn't me, Mrs Moore.'

'It wasn't you? But we were quite sure it was you. Weren't we, Lottie?' Lottie nodded. 'It looked exactly like you, Captain O'Malley.'

'Impossible.' He shook his head. 'What would I be doing in a cave?'

'That's what we were wondering. And it's why we wanted to ask you about it. But it's odd that you say you weren't there.'

'You must have mistaken me for someone else, Mrs Moore.'

'Well, yes. I suppose we must have done. Have you ever been into the cave in Smuggler's Cove?'

'No. Why would I want to go in there?'

'Well, it sounds quite exciting, if you ask me. I've heard there's a tunnel which links it to the inn.'

'It's been closed up for many years now.'

'So, there is a tunnel?'

'Yes, I believe they used it back in the olden days when there were smugglers about. But it's been closed up for at least a century. Nobody could use it now. Or so I believe. No one's got any reason to go into that cave these days, so I don't know who you saw there, Mrs Moore. Now please excuse me, I've got to take a little excursion down the coast.' He started up the boat's engine.

'Of course. See you around, Captain O'Malley!'

He unhooked the ropes, and the boat moved off.

'I think he's fibbing, Lottie, don't you? Fancy denying he was in Smuggler's Cove when we saw him there. It's so tiring when everyone lies to us!'

Chapter Forty-Five

CAPTAIN O'MALLEY ARRIVED at the next harbour on the coast about twenty minutes later. He moored his boat in the usual place and smiled when he saw the large motor car which was waiting for him. He opened the passenger door and climbed inside.

'Good morning, Captain,' said Victoria Fitzroy with a smile. 'How are you?'

'Not bad at all, Victoria. Not bad at all.'

She steered the car along the cobbles and took the road which led to the lighthouse on the headland.

'Actually, I'm a little perturbed to tell you the truth, Victoria,' he said. 'There are a couple of people who I'm struggling to understand.'

'Who?'

'The newcomers who were staying with Lady Florence. The American woman, Mrs Moore, and her assistant, Miss Sprigg. I found them very pleasant to begin with and took them on a boat trip. But there's something about them which leaves me unsure.'

'In what way?'

'They seem to be prying.'

'Into what?'

'Other people's affairs. Wherever I go, they seem to be there.'

'Such as where?'

'Smuggler's Cove. I thought I had the place to myself yesterday, but they said they saw me coming out of the cave. I didn't even notice them there.'

'What were they doing in Smuggler's Cove? It's the sort of place only locals know about.'

'Someone at Tidecrest House must have mentioned it to them.'

'And what did they see you doing?'

'Just coming out of the cave, apparently. I'd just been checking the most recent delivery.'

'So what did you say to them?'

'I denied it was me. I couldn't think of an excuse. They could only have seen me from a distance. They must have been up on the shingle path. But if they were very organised, they might have had binoculars with them.'

'Even if they did, they won't be able to guess what you were up to, will they?'

'No. But it doesn't look good. I get the feeling the pair of them are looking around for information. I suppose they want to find out who's behind Lady Florence's murder. Mrs Moore's an old friend of hers and she's understandably upset about it. But she asked me quite a few questions about Lady Florence, even after I'd tried to distract her with one of my ghost stories.'

'Oh no, not one of your ghost stories, Captain. And don't tell me you started singing a sea shanty too.'

'I was tempted to. Just to change the subject. Anyway, I'm a little worried. What will they poke their noses into next?'

They reached the lighthouse and Victoria parked the car in

the little car park. Their view was of the coastline stretching back to Fernwood-on-Sea and Shipwreck Point.

'Well, it is a worry,' said Victoria. 'But it's best to stay on friendly terms with them, I think. You know what they say. Keep your friends close and your enemies closer. I think I shall invite them to Fairhaven Manor for dinner. I don't know what Lady Florence told them about the Fitzroy family, but I can imagine it was probably unfavourable. We need to show them what nice people we are.'

'That's a good idea, Victoria. It will get them on our side, as it were. I think you can be clever about it and tell them what they want to hear. If there's an absence of information, it makes people nosy, doesn't it?'

'You're absolutely right, Captain. Leave it with me.' She smiled. 'It all could have been so different, couldn't it?'

He felt a lump in his throat. 'Yes it could have been. But no use thinking like that now, Victoria. It won't change anything.'

'No, I suppose it won't. Let's see your checklist from the cave then. I need to be sure everything has arrived.'

Chapter Forty-Six

MISS TRENT WAS red-eyed when they returned to Tidecrest House.

'Edward and I have had a terrible row!' she said.

'Oh dear,' said Mrs Moore. 'What about?'

'He's furious I told Detective Lynton I was with him at the time of Lady Florence's murder.'

'He's furious with you for telling the truth?'

'Yes! He's worried his wife is going to hear about it.'

'Well, perhaps he should have thought about that before... well, anyway. It sounds like he's being unreasonable.'

Miss Trent blew her nose. 'I think I'm beginning to realise this affair is a silly idea.'

'Is that so?'

'He's very charming and intelligent and I care about him a great deal. But he talks about money a lot. Although he earns a good salary as a doctor, I think he would rather have been born into money than have to work for it. He's envious of the aristocracy. He says he's often wished he was in the same position.'

'I'd have thought Dr Blackwood was proud to be a

doctor,' said Mrs Moore. 'How odd that he wants to be aristocratic.'

'It might be why he was attracted to Lady Florence,' said Miss Trent.

'Although Florence wasn't born into the aristocracy, was she?' said Mrs Moore. 'She married into it.'

'That was enough for him,' said Miss Trent. 'And I've been wondering recently why he's interested in me. I can understand why he was attracted to Lady Florence. She was opinionated, well-bred, well-educated, and quite handsome in her own fearsome way. But look at me. What do I have? I have little interest in nice clothes, so my appearance is often rather dowdy. I went to school, but my education wasn't remarkable. My knowledge about books, art and culture is very limited. So when you think about it like that, the two of us are really quite different. So it makes me wonder if his interest in me is for another reason.'

Lottie and Mrs Moore exchanged a glance.

'What reason?' asked Mrs Moore.

'It sounds awful to say it. But the more I think about it, the more it makes sense. Maybe he's only interested in me because I've inherited Lady Florence's estate?'

'Oh, I see. But that's only happened recently. You've been seeing Dr Blackwood for longer than that, haven't you?'

'Yes, I have. But I think Lady Florence must have told him she'd left everything in her will to me. So when he embarked on our romance, he knew that.'

'Dr Blackwood knew you were going to inherit Lady Florence's fortune?'

Miss Trent nodded. 'So I'm thinking I should perhaps put an end to it. It's been fun, but I need to remind myself that Dr Blackwood is a married man. And although he assures me his wife and he rarely talk and that he's planning to leave her, I don't want to be caught up in something like that.'

'It's also the oldest line in the book, Marianne,' said Mrs Moore. 'I don't know Dr Blackwood well enough to know if he's telling the truth or not. But many men having affairs are quite happy to assure their mistresses that they're about to leave their wives when they have no intention of doing so at all.'

'And even if he did leave her, he would only be pursuing me for my money.'

'Can you be sure about that? Perhaps he cares about you.'

'No, I think it's the money. I don't think he cares much about me at all. And the more I think about it, the angrier I get!'

The butler knocked, then stepped into the room.

'Mrs Victoria Fitzroy is here to see Mrs Moore,' he said.

'Victoria Fitzroy?' said Miss Trent. 'What does she want?' She sighed. 'I suppose you had better show her in.'

Chapter Forty-Seven

Victoria Fitzroy was shown into the room. She wore a suitably sombre day dress with a matching cloche hat over her dark, bobbed hair.

'Please forgive me for calling on you all at this difficult time. Firstly, I'd like to offer my sincerest condolences on the death of Lady Florence. Our feud was no secret, and I must add that, despite everything, I am genuinely upset about what has happened to her.'

Miss Trent pursed her lips disapprovingly.

'Lady Florence was far from perfect, but she didn't deserve to be murdered,' continued Mrs Fitzroy. 'I would like to take this opportunity to extend an olive branch.' She turned to Mrs Moore and Lottie. 'We've had no reason to fall out with each other, but I suspect your opinion of me may have been influenced by your friendship with Lady Florence.' She turned to Miss Trent. 'I think our mutual wariness of each other has been due to the feud with Lady Florence. I think it's time we put an end to it. So, I would like to invite you all to dinner at Fairhaven Manor.'

'That's very nice of you, Mrs Fitzroy,' said Mrs Moore. 'We'd be delighted to oblige.'

Miss Trent's brow furrowed. She opened her mouth, then closed it again.

'It's all I can think of to make amends,' said Mrs Fitzroy. 'I regret the feuding got as bad as it did. Lady Florence's death took me completely by surprise. You don't expect your supposed archenemy to suddenly die like that. It made me do a great deal of thinking. I would like to try and do what I can for the harmony of Fernwood-on-Sea and all the people who live here. I hope that we can all get along with each other again and forget about the unpleasantness.'

Although Lottie felt wary of Mrs Fitzroy's motive, her words seemed heartfelt.

'Hear, hear!' said Mrs Moore. 'And thank you for your conciliatory tone, Mrs Fitzroy. It's much needed in times like these.'

Mrs Fitzroy smiled. 'Thank you. I like to think so. Anyway, I shan't detain you any longer. How does Friday evening sound?'

'It sounds perfect,' said Mrs Moore.

Miss Trent opened her mouth to speak.

'What is it, Marianne?' asked Mrs Moore.

'Oh nothing. Friday is fine.'

'Wonderful!' said Mrs Fitzroy with a clap of her hands. 'I'm looking forward to it!'

The butler showed Mrs Fitzroy out and Miss Trent gave a tut. 'Don't believe a word of what Victoria Fitzroy says. She's up to something.'

'That's a shame,' said Mrs Moore. 'She seemed quite genuine to me. What could she possibly be up to?'

'If she had something to do with Lady Florence's death,

then getting everyone on her side would be the best way to evade suspicion. Think about it, if we all like her, then how can we possibly suspect her?'

'Now you put it like that, Marianne, I see what you mean. Well, there's only one way to find out how scheming she is, and that is to accept the dinner invitation. I'm quite intrigued to learn more about the Fitzroy family.'

'I shan't accept it, if that's alright,' said Miss Trent. 'I think it would be disrespectful to Lady Florence's memory.'

'Oh, I didn't mean any disrespect...'

'No, you feel free to accept the dinner invitation, Mrs Moore. I don't begrudge you for doing that. Just watch Mrs Fitzroy doesn't get her claws into you.'

Chapter Forty-Eight

'To say I'm baffled is a complete understatement, Lottie,' said Mrs Moore as they walked in the garden that afternoon with Rosie and Duke. 'I really don't understand the people here. Is it the sea air that makes them behave so unpredictably? Much as I appreciated Victoria Fitzroy's dinner invitation, I think Marianne's right that we need to be wary of her. For all we know, Mrs Fitzroy murdered Lady Florence. She could have been completely fed up with the feud, and the puncturing of her son's football might have been the last straw.'

'And so she's inviting us to dinner so we don't suspect her of doing something so dreadful,' said Lottie. 'I think she's a good suspect. But what about Lord Cavendish? He was the main suspect to begin with, and we still don't know if Detective Lynton has established an alibi for him for that evening yet.'

'Good point. It's difficult to ignore the fact that Lady Florence was murdered so soon after his return from America.'

'And he was clearly disappointed when she turned down his suggestion of a reconciliation.'

'Yes, he was. He could have attacked her out of upset and anger. But what was he doing with Dr Blackwood in The Black Anchor?'

'I don't believe he was consulting him about a medical condition,' said Lottie. 'And I didn't overhear any of their conversation because they stopped talking when I stepped through the door.'

'You've spotted Dr Blackwood with Lord Cavendish and with Arthur Harris. Are the three of them up to something?'

'Arthur Harris told Dr Blackwood that his secret was safe with him.'

'So he did! Could the secret be the affair with Marianne? Or something else? And there's Captain O'Malley to consider. He's spent most of his life at sea and claims he didn't know Lady Florence very well. But he knew her well enough to exchange greetings in the harbour on that first morning, and I think he knew her more than he's letting on. And why did he deny being at the cave in Smuggler's Cove when we saw him there? I don't understand it. Then there's the business with the rowing boat. The only rowing boat you and I have seen, Lottie, is the one that he paddles about in. And yet he denies his rowing boat was on the beach close to Lady Florence's boathouse at the time of her death.'

'But we only know it was there because Dr Blackwood mentioned it,' said Lottie. 'We don't actually have any evidence it was there.'

'True. And as for Dr Blackwood...'

'I think he's after Miss Trent's money. He could have murdered Lady Florence so Miss Trent inherited her estate. He's going to be very upset when Miss Trent tells him she wants to end the relationship.'

'Thank goodness she seems wise to him now, Lottie. And you're right, he's not going to take the news well. How is he going to get his hands on the money then? I think Dr Blackwood could be the murderer, Lottie. And we should forget about the rowing boat because Dr Blackwood invented the fact it was there to cause a distraction.'

'Perhaps he knew the mention of it would make people suspect Captain O'Malley.'

'Yes! I think that's possible. And it strikes me as off when we spotted Dr Blackwood laughing in the garden with Marianne. They were two people who were supposed to be upset about Lady Florence's death! It doesn't look good.'

'And why did Dr Blackwood arrange to walk to Shipwreck Point with Arthur Harris?' said Lottie. 'I wish I'd heard more of their conversation.'

'The pair were clearly colluding about something, and it could have been the affair with Marianne, or it could have been something else.'

Mrs Moore sighed.

'It seems everybody is acting suspiciously, Lottie. And I feel like they all know something which we don't. You and I are outsiders down here, Lottie. These people all know each other and, in some cases, have known each other for many years. It's rather difficult trying to make sense of it all. I can only hope that Detective Lynton knows what he's doing, because it's difficult to make head or tail of it. And then there's Miss Trent to consider, can we trust her yet?'

'No. I don't think we can. She may have told us about the affair with Dr Blackwood, but that doesn't mean she's being completely truthful.'

'She does a good job of tugging at the heartstrings,' said Mrs Moore. 'She knows how to cry and look sad. I'd like to think it's genuine because I sometimes feel quite sorry for her. But who can tell for sure? I'd like to know what Detective Lynton makes of everything. And I might just suggest two names to him.'

'Which ones?'

'Miss Trent and Dr Blackwood. The more I think about it, the more I think they could be in on this together. I think we need to speak to Detective Lynton and tell him our theory.'

Chapter Forty-Nine

'MISS TRENT AND DR BLACKWOOD?' said Detective Lynton. Lottie, Mrs Moore and Rosie stood with him in the wood-panelled reception area of Fernwood police station.

Mrs Moore nodded. 'And if Miss Trent is involved, then it's because Dr Blackwood pressured her into it. He wants to get his hands on the Cavendish fortune.'

Detective Lynton wiped his brow. 'Well, it's an interesting theory.'

'But you're not convinced?'

'I can't imagine either of them doing such a thing, Mrs Moore. I've known Dr Blackwood for many years and he's a much-respected gentleman in this community.'

'Is it possible that your familiarity with him could be influencing your investigation, Detective?'

'No, I like to think I'm a better detective than that.'

'And yet you describe him as a much-respected gentleman which suggests you don't believe he's capable of such a thing.'

'It's a struggle to believe that anyone in this village is capable of such a thing, and yet I must consider them all. So—'

The ringing telephone on the police station desk interrupted them. The desk sergeant answered it. His face swiftly grew serious as he listened.

'Very well,' he said. 'We'll get there right away.'

'What is it, Parkinson?' asked the detective.

'Someone's fallen off the cliff at Shipwreck Point.'

'Good grief, that sounds serious. Has the coastguard been summoned?'

'Yes, but we're needed too, sir. A witness in a boat says they saw two people at the top of the cliff and they believe the person was pushed.'

Mrs Moore clasped a hand over her mouth. 'How horrible!'

Chapter Fifty

'Poor Dr Blackwood!' wailed Miss Trent. 'He didn't deserve it!'

Mrs Moore, Lottie and Rosie sat with her in the sitting room of Tidecrest House. Mrs Moore perched on the arm of Miss Trent's chair and patted her shoulder. 'It's dreadful, Marianne.'

'Who could have done this to him?'

'I'm sure the police will find out.'

'I don't understand it! Oh, I feel so awful now. I told him I wanted to end our affair and now he's dead!'

The butler stepped into the room with Detective Lynton.

'Hello again, Mrs Moore and Miss Sprigg,' said the detective. 'I'm sorry to intrude, Miss Trent, but I must ask a few questions.'

She gave a sad nod and blew her nose.

The detective sat in an armchair and took out his notebook. 'When did you last see Dr Blackwood?' he asked.

'This afternoon. He called in here on his walk to Shipwreck Point.'

'What time was that?'

'About three o'clock. It was after Mrs Fitzroy visited. Mrs Moore and Miss Sprigg were out in the garden.'

The detective turned to them. 'Did you see Dr Blackwood?'

'No,' said Mrs Moore. 'We were in the garden and then decided to walk to the village to speak to you.'

'How long was Dr Blackwood here for, Miss Trent?' asked the detective.

'Not long. He left quite quickly because...'

'Because what?'

'I had to give him some bad news.'

'What sort of bad news?'

'I'd realised our affair was a mistake. And so I told him it was over.'

'How did he take the news?'

'He was unhappy about it. But I don't believe it's because he loved me. I don't think he loved me at all. I think he wanted to get his hands on this house and estate. I think he was planning to leave his wife and marry me. But he was only interested in my wealth.'

'Interesting,' said the detective. 'And after he went on his way, what did you do, Miss Trent?'

'I stayed here, pottering about.'

'Can other people vouch for that?'

'Oh, Detective! You're not suggesting I had something to do with his death, are you? I couldn't push anyone off a cliff. It's a horrific thing to do!'

'Do you have an alibi for the time that Dr Blackwood fell from the cliff?'

'Oh no, not this again!' She slumped forward with her head in her hands.

'What time did Dr Blackwood fall from the cliff?' Mrs Moore asked Detective Lynton.

'The witness in the boat says it was about four o'clock.'

'So an hour after Dr Blackwood called at the house.'

Lottie considered this. Miss Trent could have accompanied him to Shipwreck Point. She shuddered as she thought of the narrow path and its proximity to the cliff edge. It would be easy to nudge someone off if they weren't expecting it.

'Miss Trent,' said the detective. 'I realise this is a difficult time for you, but it's extremely important that you tell me where you were at four o'clock this afternoon.'

Chapter Fifty-One

Fairhaven Manor was an impressive grey stone manor house set in lush green parkland.

'I can't say I'm in the mood for socialising, Lottie,' said Mrs Moore as Langley halted the car by the manor's columned porch. 'But I'm too curious about the Fitzroy family to cancel the dinner invitation.'

She was wearing a midnight blue satin gown which was quite understated for her usual evening attire.

A liveried footman opened the car doors for them. They were shown into the grand entrance hall where Victoria Fitzroy was descending the grand staircase. Her sequinned dress sparkled as much as the chandeliers above their heads. Rosie greeted her, and she patted the corgi on the head.

'Thank you for coming!' she said with a smile. 'I realise it's a difficult time for you at the moment. How's Miss Trent faring?'

'I'm afraid she's rather unhappy,' said Mrs Moore.

'Oh dear. There's little comfort in a police cell, is there?'

Miss Trent had been in police custody for two days. Detective Lynton had arrested her because she'd been unable to account for her whereabouts at the time of Dr Blackwood's murder.

Lord and Lady Fitzroy awaited them in the drawing room. Lord Fitzroy was a refined elderly gentleman with grey hair and a neat moustache. His wife had a haughty appearance and silvery hair which was pinned neatly on top of her head. She wore a gown of dark violet.

'It's a pleasure to meet you, Mrs Moore,' said Lord Fitzroy. 'I've already heard quite a lot about you.'

'Have you, my lord? News travels fast.'

'In a place like Fernwood-on-Sea, it does,' said Lady Fitzroy.

'We hear you're from a wealthy American family,' said her husband.

'Yes, that's right,' said Mrs Moore. 'My father was a railroad magnate in Pennsylvania.'

'Do you go back there often?' asked Lady Fitzroy.

'No, I haven't spent a lot of time there recently. I have a townhouse in London, and I also enjoy travelling. My sister lives in England too. She's married to Lord Buckley-Phipps.'

'Buckley-Phipps?' said Lord Fitzroy. 'Fine fellow. I believe we frequent the same club in London.'

'Do you really? It's a small world.'

'The aristocracy is a small world,' said Lady Fitzroy with a thin smile. 'But the rest of it is quite large.'

A footman served them glasses of champagne from a silver tray.

'It would be remiss of us if we didn't pass on our condolences to you on the sad passing of your friend, Lady Florence,' said Lady Fitzroy. 'We were saddened to hear about it.'

'Thank you, my lady,' said Mrs Moore.

'And it looks like the maid did it!' said Lord Fitzroy. 'Shocking.'

'Companion,' said Lady Fitzroy. 'Miss Trent was more than a maid.'

'I don't think we know yet whether Miss Trent murdered Lady Florence,' said Mrs Fitzroy. 'But she pushed Dr Blackwood off the cliff.'

'I don't think we know that either,' said Mrs Moore. 'She's merely suspected of doing it.'

'Well, she must have done something wrong, otherwise they wouldn't have arrested her,' said Lord Fitzroy. 'It looked like she'd done alright to begin with, didn't it? Inherited the entire estate.'

'Lord Cavendish must be absolutely seething,' said Lady Fitzroy. 'He didn't get a very good deal from the divorce. Then he went to America, lost all his money, came back again, and now his former wife's dead and Miss Trent owns everything.'

'But she ruined it for herself by murdering people,' said Lord Fitzroy.

'There's no evidence that she murdered anyone,' said Mrs Moore.

'What happens when she's in prison?' said Lord Fitzroy, ignoring Mrs Moore's comment. 'Presumably the estate will have to go to someone else. You can't have a prisoner owning that house and all that land.'

'Perhaps Cavendish will get it off her,' said Lady Fitzroy.

'You think he will?'

'I don't know. It's all quite unprecedented.'

The bell rang for dinner, and they rose and made their way to the dining room. It had deep red walls and large paintings in heavy frames. Glittering silver and glass tableware was laid out on a pristine white tablecloth.

They talked about the weather while the spring vegetable soup was served. Lottie began to feel a little bored until Mrs Moore asked a question, 'Forgive me for the directness of my question, but I'd like to learn more about your feud with Lady Florence.'

Mrs Fitzroy sighed. 'We just didn't see eye-to-eye.'

'She was querulous and truculent,' said Lord Fitzroy.

'We all tried to get along with her,' said his wife. 'But I'm afraid it was a bit of a lost cause.'

'It even got too much for Miss Trent,' said Lord Fitzroy. 'That's why she murdered her.'

'We don't know that to be the case yet, Harold,' said his wife.

'Who else could it have been?' said Lord Fitzroy.

'There are some other possibilities,' said Mrs Moore. 'A rowing boat was seen on the beach at the time of Lady Florence's death,' said Mrs Moore. 'The only person I know who has a rowing boat is Captain O'Malley.'

'Lots of people have rowing boats here,' said Mrs Fitzroy.

'O'Malley would never have done it,' said Lord Fitzroy.

'If it wasn't Miss Trent, then it was clearly someone she had upset,' said Lady Fitzroy. 'I believe you witnessed yourself, Mrs Moore, the cruelty she inflicted upon my poor grandson by deflating his football. That was the sort of thing she did. And I should think in the end she did it one too many times and someone snapped.'

'Do you know if she fell out with Captain O'Malley?' asked Mrs Moore.

'Captain O'Malley had nothing to do with it!' said Mrs Fitzroy. The forcefulness of her response stunned the table into silence. 'Oh, I do apologise,' she said, laying down her soup spoon. 'There's something I should tell you, Mrs Moore. Captain O'Malley is my uncle.'

Lottie felt her jaw drop.

'Your uncle, Mrs Fitzroy? I see.'

'He's always been very kind to me. My parents were young when they both died, and Captain O'Malley and his sister took me in. Unfortunately, he was away at sea a lot and so I was brought up by my aunt. I don't think she cared for children a great deal. But when my uncle was home, I would spend time with him.'

'Well, that's very interesting to hear, Mrs Fitzroy.'

'Captain O'Malley is the closest family member I have now. My aunt died some years ago.'

'It must be nice to have him nearby now.'

'Yes, it is.' She smiled. 'He's quite an eccentric local character, but he's very fond of me, and I'm very fond of him.'

'Well, it's certainly interesting coming to a place like this as an outsider,' said Mrs Moore. 'Because one really has no idea of what connection various people have with each other. So it's both a surprise and quite delightful to discover these things. I understand now why you won't consider he played a part in Lady Florence's death. I can only apologise for mentioning the rowing boat.'

'It's quite alright, Mrs Moore. You weren't to know.'

'As for Lady Florence,' said Lord Fitzroy. 'I think she would have chipped away at someone and driven them half-mad. In the end, they couldn't control their anger for a moment longer.'

Lottie noticed Mrs Fitzroy looking rather pale.

Lady Fitzroy appeared to have noticed it, too. 'Are you alright, Victoria?'

'I need to excuse myself for a moment. I'm feeling a little lightheaded.'

'Oh dear. Yes, please do get some rest.'

A maid came to Mrs Fitzroy's aid and helped her from the room.

Chapter Fifty-Two

LOTTIE, Mrs Moore and Rosie called in at the Fernwood-on-Sea police station the following morning.

'We're here about Miss Trent,' said Mrs Moore. 'Would it be possible to see her?'

'I'll check with Detective Lynton,' said the desk sergeant. He returned a short while later with the detective and a miserable-looking Miss Trent.

'Oh, Mrs Moore!' She flung herself at her. 'Please take me home!'

'You're free to go, Marianne?' said Mrs Moore, putting a comforting arm around her.

Detective Lynton nodded. 'I've been trying my hardest to find some evidence that Miss Trent was on that cliff edge with Dr Blackwood, but I haven't got anywhere.'

'Because I wasn't there!' wailed Miss Trent.

'Alright Marianne,' said Mrs Moore. 'Let's get you home.'

Miss Trent seemed a little happier after some coffee and cakes on the terrace at Tidecrest House.

'I suppose the police are only doing their job,' she said. 'But they've wasted so much of their time on me I'm worried the murderer has got clean away!'

'It's a tough case for Detective Lynton,' said Mrs Moore. 'And I really don't know how he's going to solve this. Who could possibly have murdered Dr Blackwood and why?'

'I don't know,' said Miss Trent sadly. 'I suppose that's why I was arrested. They couldn't think of any other suspects.'

'Dr Blackwood's wife?'

'Maybe.' Miss Trent shrugged. 'But his death has to be connected to Lady Florence's, doesn't it? I can't see why Mrs Blackwood would want to murder Lady Florence. And if she murdered her husband but not Lady Florence, that means we have two murderers in Fernwood-on-Sea! That seems impossible in a place where nothing like this has ever happened before.'

'It's a puzzle,' said Mrs Moore. 'And I can't stop thinking about that rowing boat. Captain O'Malley has to have had something to do with this. Did he know Dr Blackwood?'

'Yes, they knew each other. But they weren't friends. They weren't enemies, either. They had little to do with each other.'

'Lottie and I saw Captain O'Malley coming out of the cave in Smuggler's Cove,' said Mrs Moore.

'Really?' Miss Trent's eyes widened. 'The old cave which smugglers used to use?'

'Yes. Do you think he could be a smuggler?'

'I really don't know. I've not given it a thought before. But why else would he be in the old cave? There's a tunnel which connects it to The Black Anchor inn.'

'And Lottie saw Dr Blackwood with Lord Cavendish in that inn a few evenings ago.'

'Is that so? Well Edward never mentioned that to me.'

'You don't know why they would have met?'

'No.'

'Lord Cavendish told me he was consulting Dr Blackwood about a medical condition,' said Lottie.

'In The Black Anchor?'

'Yes. It's a strange location for a medical consultation,' said Mrs Moore.

'I'm not sure Lord Cavendish was telling me the truth,' said Lottie. 'But if he and Dr Blackwood were in the inn and Captain O'Malley was in the cave, perhaps they were all involved in a smuggling operation.'

Miss Trent gasped. 'You think so? Edward never mentioned it, but then he wouldn't mention something like that.'

'Perhaps it's the reason behind Dr Blackwood's murder?' said Lottie. 'Maybe he fell out with the other two about the smuggling.'

'Or he accidentally found out about it while he was at The Black Anchor,' said Miss Trent. 'And so they murdered him to keep him quiet! And maybe Lady Florence found out about it, too? Could that be the reason she was murdered? Gosh. I can't believe Lord Cavendish and Captain O'Malley could be behind this.'

'And we only discovered yesterday evening that Captain O'Malley is Victoria Fitzroy's uncle,' said Mrs Moore.

'Yes, that's right.'

'You knew that?'

'Yes. Did I not mention it to you? I apologise if I didn't. I suppose I know quite a lot about everyone in the village, so I didn't think to mention it. She was visiting her uncle in the village when she met the young Jasper Fitzroy. They had a courtship, then married, and that was how she became part of the Fitzroy family. There's not a lot of similarity between Captain O'Malley and his niece, is there?'

'No. Not much at all. I just assumed she was from an aristocratic family like her husband.'

'No. Although she saw little of him when she was growing up. She was raised by an aunt while he was away at sea.' Miss Trent sipped her coffee and thought for a moment. 'The idea of a smuggling ring intrigues me. I know Victoria Fitzroy and her uncle are quite close. Could she be in on it, too?'

Chapter Fifty-Three

'YES!' said Mrs Moore. 'I think we've solved it!'

'Really?' said Lottie.

'Yes. It's quite obvious, isn't it? Lady Florence and Dr Blackwood found out about the smuggling operation being carried out by Captain O'Malley, Lord Cavendish and Mrs Fitzroy.'

'But Lord Cavendish has only just returned from America,' said Lottie. 'How could he have got involved so quickly with the smuggling ring?'

'By all accounts, he was desperate for money, Lottie. We've heard how he lost his money in America and came back here hoping to reconcile with Lady Florence and have access to her fortune. But she said no, and he was probably desperate. Perhaps he knew Captain O'Malley was a smuggler and asked if he could be involved.'

'It makes sense,' said Miss Trent. 'And it explains why Captain O'Malley's rowing boat was on the beach when Lady Florence was murdered. And then Mrs Fitzroy pushed Dr Blackwood off the cliff.'

'Why Mrs Fitzroy?' asked Lottie.

'Because she called in here to invite us to dinner at Fairhaven Manor earlier that same afternoon. You both went for a walk, and then Dr Blackwood called in. She must have seen him arrive at the house and decided to follow him. He could have been pushed by Captain O'Malley or Lord Cavendish, but I think it's most likely Mrs Fitzroy did it.'

'Detective Lynton will be able to establish alibis for them,' said Mrs Moore. 'Or not, as may be the case. Why don't we telephone him and tell him what we know? Then he can investigate further.'

'Would you mind telephoning him, Mrs Moore?' asked Miss Trent. 'I don't think I'd like to speak to him so soon after my ordeal in the police cells.'

'Of course, Marianne. I'll telephone him now.'

'You can use the telephone in the study.'

Mrs Moore left the room and Duke followed her.

Lottie didn't feel convinced by the theory. There were too many thoughts in her mind which didn't fit. Snippets of conversations and ideas which pointed elsewhere.

A short while later, Mrs Moore returned. 'Detective Lynton says he'll look into it,' she said. 'He's going to send some men to the cave and then he'd like to hold a gathering here tomorrow morning to discuss it further.'

'Here?' said Miss Trent.

'Well, I agreed because you have plenty of space here, Marianne. Would you prefer if I told him it's not convenient?'

'No. Here is fine.'

If Mrs Moore and Miss Trent were mistaken, Lottie realised she had little time to come up with an alternative idea. A thought had been weighing on her mind for a little while and now was the time to act on it.

'I'm going to walk down to the village,' she said.

'Now?' said Mrs Moore. 'But it's nearly lunchtime.'

'Oh, that's alright. I'll get something to eat while I'm there.'

Chapter Fifty-Four

Detective Lynton arrived at Tidecrest House at eleven o'clock the following morning.

'Thank you for your telephone call yesterday, Mrs Moore,' he said. 'You'll be pleased to hear that the information you provided me with led us to an important discovery.'

'Really? What is it, Detective?'

'I'll make an announcement once everyone's here.'

'Everyone?'

'Yes, I've invited some other people to join us.' He turned to Miss Trent. 'I'd like all the household staff present too. Can we use the drawing room?'

'Yes, I suppose so,' said Miss Trent. 'Can't you tell us what you've found?'

'I could, but I don't want to waste time repeating myself. Let's wait until everyone's arrived.'

Tilly the maid arranged the chairs in the drawing room so they faced the fireplace. The butler and the housekeeper fetched some extra chairs from the dining room.

Captain O'Malley was the first to arrive. 'What's all this about, Miss Trent?' he asked.

MARTHA BOND

'Detective Lynton has an announcement to make.'

'What sort of announcement?'

'I don't know, he won't tell us.'

Lord Cavendish arrived next. 'You're a free woman again, Miss Trent,' he said.

'Yes. I've done nothing wrong.'

'Is that so? Why were you arrested then?'

'You'll have to ask the detective about that.'

'I will. But you know what they say. No smoke without fire.'

He went off to take a seat and Miss Trent gave him a sharp stare.

Detective Lynton took up position in front of the fire-place. 'Is everyone here?' he said.

Lottie noticed a sergeant and two constables had also arrived. They stood at the side of the room.

The butler stepped into the room with three more people. Victoria Fitzroy and Lord and Lady Fitzroy.

'Everyone must be here now,' said the detective. 'I'll begin. We're here today because I received a tip-off yesterday from someone who shall remain anonymous. I was told about a possible modern-day smuggling operation in Fern-wood-on-Sea and I was given names. I wasn't sure whether to believe it at first, but Sergeant Grigson took some men down to Smuggler's Cove and found some interesting items in a cave there.'

'What?' said Lord Cavendish.

'Seven tea chests,' said the detective. 'Four of them contained brandy, whisky and rum. Three contained tobacco. Sergeant Grigson also discovered that the tunnel between the cave and The Black Anchor has been put into use again. It was blocked off fifty years ago to prevent smugglers from using the cove, but someone has reopened it.'

He was met with silence, and Lottie felt like she was in a

180

classroom with a teacher asking someone to own up for a misdeed.

'It appears no one wishes to provide me with more detail,' said Detective Lynton. 'But I've been given names of various individuals. I know who to speak to.'

'I know what this is about,' said Captain O'Malley. 'Mrs Moore and Miss Sprigg saw me by the cave the other day. They've told you about it, haven't they?'

Lottie felt her face redden at the mention of her name.

'I couldn't possibly say,' said the detective. 'But there's little doubt the cave was being used for nefarious purposes. Someone has shipped in those tea chests to avoid paying customs duty. They presumably then hawk their wares locally to make a tidy profit. My men will be able to establish exactly who these smugglers are. Especially now the landlord of The Black Anchor has been arrested. There really is no place to hide.'

Captain O'Malley cleared his throat. 'What if I admitted it all to save you time, Detective? There's no smuggling operation. It's just me. On my own.'

Lottie noticed his niece, Mrs Fitzroy, give him a surprised look.

'Just me, Detective,' continued Captain O'Malley. 'So you can arrest me now and everyone else can get on with their day. I don't understand why you summoned everyone up to Tidecrest House just for this.'

'Well, there's another matter too,' said Detective Lynton. 'A matter of murder.'

'Murder?' said Captain O'Malley. 'No. I'll admit to the smuggling. But I had nothing to do with murder.'

'There's a reason Lady Florence and Dr Blackwood were murdered,' said Detective Lynton. 'They found out about your smuggling operation, Captain O'Malley. And you murdered them!'

'Me? No!' He glanced around the room, as if looking for assistance.

'Lady Florence threatened to tell, didn't she?' said Detective Lynton.

'No,' said Captain O'Malley. 'You're making a mistake, Detective! Lady Florence didn't find out about it at all. She never mentioned it to me, nor did she threaten to tell anyone.'

'That's why your rowing boat was seen on the beach at the time of her death, wasn't it? And who spotted that boat? Dr Blackwood. Not only had he implicated you in the murder of Lady Florence, but he also knew you were a smuggler!'

'No!' said Captain O'Malley. 'None of this is true!'

Lottie realised it was time to put forward her idea. She couldn't be completely sure she was correct, but she had to try.

She took in a breath and got to her feet.

'Miss Sprigg?' said Detective Lynton. 'You have something to say?'

'Yes,' said Lottie. 'I think I know who the murderer is.'

Chapter Fifty-Five

'THE OBVIOUS CULPRIT at the beginning was Lord Cavendish,' said Lottie. 'Lady Florence's murder coincided with his return from America. He didn't fully explain why he'd come back, but everyone assumed it was because he'd lost all his money over there and wanted to return to the place he'd once called home. As part of the divorce settlement, Lady Florence was entitled to live in this house. This didn't appear to be a problem initially because Lord Cavendish left for America to start a new life. But when that didn't work out for him, he returned to England hoping to reconcile with his former wife.'

'Is that a fair assessment, my lord?' Detective Lynton asked Lord Cavendish.

'She may be a young girl, but it is. You've got an old head on young shoulders, Miss Sprigg. What do you know about broken hearts and divorce?'

'Not a great deal,' said Lottie. 'But I watched and listened and learned that way.'

'I'd like to correct something, though,' said Lord

Cavendish. 'I didn't lose all of my money in America. Just most of it.'

'Very well,' said the detective. 'And you're not involved in the smuggling operation?'

'No! I know nothing about that.'

'I saw you in The Black Anchor, my lord,' said Lottie. 'I wondered then if you had something to do with smuggling.'

'No. I was there to discuss a medical condition with Dr Blackwood. He was the one who suggested the location.'

'Why not his surgery?' asked the detective.

'I didn't want to be seen going there. When you're as well-known as me in the village, people tend to talk when they see you at the doctor's surgery. People were already talking about me as it was. They all thought I murdered my dear old wife!'

'Former wife.'

'I can't tell you how broken-hearted I was when Florence was murdered. We may have been divorced, but I never stopped loving her. And that's why I had hoped for a reconciliation. It wasn't just about the money and the house. Although I admit I missed those things, and I did want them back again. But I also wanted Florence back. I had made a mistake.' He shook his head in dismay. 'I was foolish to think she'd want to take me back. And that's the conversation you witnessed between us, Miss Sprigg and Mrs Moore. I had suggested that we get back together and her answer was no. The idea that I would then murder her out of revenge is dreadful! Extremely upsetting. And what would I have gained from it, anyway? I knew that Florence had left everything to Marianne in her will. So murdering my wife would not have meant I was entitled to any of her riches.'

'So you think Lord Cavendish is innocent, Miss Sprigg?' asked Detective Lynton.

'Yes, quite sure. But then I wondered if the murderer could have been Miss Trent.'

'Me?' said Miss Trent. 'Oh, not again!'

'I didn't want to suspect you,' said Lottie. 'But we were confused by the way you suddenly left the dining table on the evening of Lady Florence's death. You said you tried to make a telephone call and tidied the study. You were missing for an hour.'

'I don't know how you could have thought that,' said Miss Trent. 'What motive could I possibly have had?'

'All I could think of was that you wanted to get your hands on the house and money sooner rather than later,' said Lottie. 'But once we found out about your affair with Dr Blackwood, I wondered if he could have been involved too.'

'Really?' said Detective Lynton.

'Yes, I wondered for a short while if Miss Trent and Dr Blackwood had colluded to get their hands on Lady Florence's estate.'

'I can see why you thought that, Miss Sprigg,' said Miss Trent. 'I realise now how foolish I was to have a love affair with Dr Blackwood. He was only interested in the money!'

'Is that so?' said the detective.

'Many people thought he was a respectable man,' said Miss Trent. 'But he was impressed with wealth and status and did all he could to obtain it. He didn't murder Lady Florence though because I was with him at the time of her death. We had arranged to meet in the garden that evening and that's why I was apparently missing for about an hour. He'd sworn me to secrecy because he was married. I realised in the end that I had to confess to the affair so he could provide an alibi!'

'So it wasn't Miss Trent, Miss Sprigg,' said Detective Lynton. 'So who do you think it is?'

'I considered other people. And Victoria Fitzroy was an obvious choice.'

'Me?' said Mrs Fitzroy.

'You had a feud with Lady Florence,' said Lottie. 'And I

saw how Lady Florence punctured your son's football during our picnic on Windy Edge. It was a cruel thing to do, and I can understand why you'd be upset about it.'

'Yes, I was. It was completely uncalled for. I'm afraid that's the sort of person she was. I'm sure it would have shocked you at the time, Miss Sprigg. But to be honest with you, I was quite used to her behaviour.'

'I wondered if a member of the Fitzroy family could have got to Lady Florence's boathouse that fateful night without being seen,' continued Lottie. 'But no one spotted them anywhere near the beach that evening. So although I could find a motive for why Mrs Fitzroy would want to murder Lady Florence, I couldn't understand how she would have managed it. Unless you got there by rowing boat, Mrs Fitzroy.'

'Dr Blackwood could have invented the rowing boat,' said Mrs Fitzroy. 'There's no evidence it was there. And I think we all realise now what a duplicitous man he was.'

'Well, I believed he was telling the truth,' said Detective Lynton. 'And we've tried all we can to find the owner. It could have belonged to Captain O'Malley, or it could have belonged to someone else.' He flicked through his notebook. 'That said, I don't think you ever provided an alibi for your whereabouts that evening, Captain O'Malley.'

'No. Because I was on my boat. Alone. It can't be helped. I spend a lot of time on my boat alone. It's what I'm used to. So as much as I would like to give you an alibi, Detective, I can't.'

'But isn't it about time, Captain O'Malley?' said Mrs Fitzroy.

He gave her a wary glance. 'About time for what?'

'We've been over this so many times. And I really believe some things have to be resolved now. Isn't it about time you finally told the truth?'

Chapter Fifty-Six

CAPTAIN O'MALLEY FOLDED HIS ARMS.

'No, Victoria. I don't believe it is time to tell the truth.'

'But wouldn't it just be easier? I'm so sick of hiding secrets all the time. It wears me down. It's exhausting.'

'I don't find it exhausting.'

'But I do! Can't you at least help me? Perhaps you're happy to go to your grave with secrets. Lady Florence certainly did. But wouldn't life just be easier if the secrets came out?'

Captain O'Malley gazed up at the ceiling and ran a hand over his beard.

'Please,' said Mrs Fitzroy. 'Just explain everything. And then everyone will know why your rowing boat was on the beach that evening.'

There was a hushed silence in the room. The only sound was Captain O'Malley scratching his whiskers.

Everyone waited patiently as he cleared his throat and refolded his arms. 'Why now, Victoria?'

'Why not now? An awful lot has happened. Two people have been murdered. Nothing has ever occurred like this in

Fernwood-on-Sea before. It's the right time to tell everyone. Then we can make a fresh start.'

He sighed and got to his feet. 'Very well. But I'm doing this for you, Victoria, no one else.'

'Thank you.' She clasped her hands at her chest in gratitude.

The captain took in a breath and began, 'I first met Florence a little over thirty years ago,' he said. 'She was Florence Davis back then. A young woman from London who'd fallen out with her family and had come to live by the sea. She was an attractive young lady. And I should add that I was a young man at the time, too. Not particularly attractive, though. Florence wanted to learn how to sail and I didn't hesitate to offer her a few lessons.

'We got on well. In fact, we got on a little too well for our own good. And there was a romance between us. It was short-lived because I had to go away to sea with the navy. So that's what I did. She didn't want me to go. But it was my job, and off I went. I was away for about a year. When I returned to Fernwood, I was looking forward to seeing Florence again. But there was no sign of her. I didn't know where she'd gone.

'Then, late one evening, there was a knock at the door. I answered to find Florence there holding a baby. It was a little girl, about six months old. Florence was in a state. She told me she'd had to go away and have the baby in secret. She couldn't let anyone know what had happened because it would forever be a stain on her character. She told me she was getting the baby adopted. I didn't want that to happen. I offered to marry her, but she turned me down. I couldn't bear the thought of not seeing my young daughter again, so I told Florence I'd ask my sister, Matilda, to look after the baby.

'Florence handed me the baby there and then. And she left. I later learned she went back up to London to find herself a fancy husband. I wasn't good enough for her.' He shook his head. 'Thankfully, Matilda and her husband agreed to look after the baby. We invented a story that a sister of ours and her husband had died suddenly. We explained that's where the baby had come from, and surprisingly few people questioned it. From that moment onwards, I thought of that girl as my niece.'

There were gasps. Mrs Fitzroy's face was mask-like as she tried to keep her emotions under control.

'So Victoria Fitzroy isn't your niece,' said the detective. 'She's your daughter?'

'She is,' Captain O'Malley gave a firm nod. 'And I'm extremely proud of her, too. She's grown into a fine young woman.'

Mrs Fitzroy let out a sob and clasped a handkerchief to her face.

'Well, I never!' exclaimed Lord Fitzroy.

'No!' Lord Cavendish jumped to his feet. 'This is all wrong. Florence never had a child. She didn't want children!'

Chapter Fifty-Seven

'No, Florence didn't want children, Lord Cavendish,' said Captain O'Malley. 'But she had a child, all the same.'

'No. She would have told me this! Florence and I knew everything about each other!'

'I'm afraid you didn't,' said Captain O'Malley. 'And I'm sure you would never have married her if you'd known she'd had an illegitimate child.'

'I would have. I loved her.'

Captain O'Malley shook his head. 'No, you wouldn't, Lord Cavendish. You may have loved her, but there would have been too much shame associated with marrying her. She kept quiet about it, and everyone can understand why. It was her greatest fear that people would find out.'

Detective Lynton turned to Mrs Fitzroy. 'How long have you known that Captain O'Malley was your father?'

'He told me when I was fourteen,' she said, wiping her nose. 'He wanted to make sure I was old enough to understand. I had always called him uncle, and I remembered him visiting when I was very young. I knew he went away a lot to sea. But whenever he was home, he would always call on me. I enjoyed his visits.' She smiled. 'When he told me the truth about my parents, Lady Florence was very unhappy about it.'

'She was,' said Captain O'Malley. 'She was very angry indeed. But I told her the young woman needed to know the truth. I didn't want to lie to my daughter. I always felt she should know exactly where she was from.'

'I tried to get along with my mother,' said Mrs Fitzroy. 'But I couldn't. I think she resented me. And I think she was fearful that people would find out I was her daughter. It would have quite ruined her. So I wasn't able to see much of her. I don't think she ever really wanted to acknowledge me as her daughter. But she came to my wedding to Mr Fitzroy. That's because everybody in the village was invited. She wasn't happy I married into the Fitzroy family. A family she had feuded with over the years.'

'But we welcomed you with open arms,' said Lady Fitzroy. 'You made our dear Jasper very happy indeed.'

'Why did Lady Florence come back to Fernwood-on-Sea if she didn't want to be associated with you, Mrs Fitzroy?' asked the detective.

'I think she probably wanted to keep an eye on me from afar. And when old Mrs Harmsworth died and left Tidecrest House, the opportunity to buy it was too good to be true for her. She had everything she wanted then. She lived in a beautiful home which everyone was envious of, and she was married to a lord.'

'I'm still struggling to believe this,' said Lord Cavendish. 'How I wish Florence had told me!'

'It was hard to accept my mother was an unlikeable person,' said Mrs Fitzroy. 'But parents aren't always perfect, are they? My mother was only really interested in herself.'

'So your son, Mrs Fitzroy,' said Mrs Moore. 'The young man who kicked his ball into our picnic. He's Lady Florence's grandson?'

Victoria nodded sadly. 'Yes. And she deliberately punctured his football. I don't think many grandmothers would have done that. But she had very little to do with him.'

'Golly,' said Mrs Moore.

'And perhaps you can explain now, Captain O'Malley, why your rowing boat was on the beach that evening,' said Mrs Fitzroy.

'Well, yes. That was my rowing boat on the beach,' he said. 'I admit it now. Why not? All the secrets are coming out now. I went to see Lady Florence because I was very angry when I heard what she'd done to our grandson's ball. Although Victoria said she was used to Lady Florence behaving like that, she was still upset about it. And when she told me about it, I was furious. So I hopped into my boat and rowed to the beach. And I saw her there, heading for the boathouse. I guessed she would be going out for a sail that evening.

'She didn't want to talk to me, of course. She didn't want to be associated with me. But I insisted on it. I demanded to know why she'd punctured our grandson's ball. She told me he had ruined her chicken pie. I told her that if I'd been there, I'd have picked up that chicken pie and squashed it into her face. Well, she didn't like that at all. She marched off to the boathouse, and I followed her. And in the boathouse, we had a terrible row. She closed the door because she didn't want anyone to hear. Perhaps that's when Dr Blackwood walked past and spotted my boat there. How he didn't hear us shouting at each other, I don't know. Maybe the sound of the waves drowned out the noise. Anyway, she wouldn't admit she'd done anything wrong. And she didn't want to apologise for it. So I left her.'

'You didn't...?' asked the detective.

'Murder her?' said Captain O'Malley. 'No, I didn't. I didn't lay a finger on her. I wanted to, mind you. But I've never hit a woman in my life. I never have and I never will. I'll happily hit a man. But never a woman. I left that boathouse, returned to my boat, and rowed back to the harbour. And that's the honest truth. I have nothing more to add.'

Mrs Fitzroy got up, stepped over to him, and gave him an embrace. 'Thank you, Captain,' she said. 'I feel better now that everyone knows. They can judge us as much as they like. But at least I won't have to keep the secret anymore.'

He blinked a few times, then wiped his eyes. 'Perhaps you can call me Father now, Victoria.'

Chapter Fifty-Eight

LOTTIE HADN'T EXPECTED to hear the revelation that Captain O'Malley and Lady Florence were Victoria Fitzroy's parents. She thought back to how evasive Captain O'Malley had been when Mrs Moore had asked him about Lady Florence. She also thought of how Victoria Fitzroy had abruptly left the dinner table when people were talking about Lady Florence. She'd presumably found some conversations about her mother difficult to listen to. Lottie felt sympathy for Victoria Fitzroy. She had never had a proper relationship with her mother. Thankfully, she appeared to have had a good relationship with her father. Even if they had needed to pretend to everyone that they were uncle and niece.

Seeing the father and daughter embrace made Lottie think for a moment about her own parents.

She didn't know who they were, and she hadn't even replied to Josephine Holmes's letter yet. What would Miss Holmes think of her for being so slow to reply?

It took a moment for her to realise Detective Lynton was speaking to her.

'I'm sorry?' she said.

'Have you got anything else to say, Miss Sprigg? You mentioned you might know who the murderer is.'

'Oh yes.'

'So who is it?'

Lottie began again. 'There's someone we haven't discussed yet,' she said, 'and that's Arthur Harris.'

Arthur Harris had been sitting quietly at the back of the room, wearing his scruffy overalls. He gave Lottie a curious glance.

'Arthur?' said the detective. 'One of Lady Florence's most loyal employees?'

'And I won't hear a word against him!' said Miss Trent. 'He's had a very difficult time recently.'

'Yes, he has,' said Lottie. 'But that doesn't excuse the murder of two people.'

'Just a moment, Miss Sprigg,' said Detective Lynton. 'Are you accusing Arthur of murder?'

Lottie nodded. 'I am. I can't help thinking about a conversation I heard between Arthur Harris and Dr Blackwood on Shipwreck Point.'

'How did you hear our conversation?' asked Arthur.

'I hadn't planned to eavesdrop. I was in the church while the pair of you were sitting on the bench.'

'You thought you could spy on us?'

'I didn't plan to. It was while I was in the church that I realised I could hear your conversation through the window. I heard the pair of you agree to hide some information so the police wouldn't get distracted by it. And then you told Dr Blackwood that his secret was safe with you.'

'Is that a fair recollection, Mr Harris?' asked Detective Lynton.

'I can't remember what we were talking about.'

'Does it sound familiar?'

'No.'

'It sounds like you misheard, Miss Sprigg,' said Detective Lynton.

'I don't think I did.'

'So what was the secret?' said the detective.

'I think it was Dr Blackwood's affair with Marianne Trent,' said Lottie. 'And I suspect Arthur and Dr Blackwood bumped into each other on the evening Lady Florence was murdered. Dr Blackwood would have needed to walk from the beach to the garden to meet Miss Trent. He wanted to keep the encounter secret for obvious reasons. And I think Mr Harris saw him.'

'But Mr Harris was having tea with his family at that time,' said the detective.

'That's what his wife says,' said Lottie. 'But he could have asked her to say that.'

'Why would she lie?'

'Because I think Mr Harris went to the boathouse after his tea and murdered Lady Florence. On his way there, he bumped into Dr Blackwood. Neither man wanted anyone to know they were there. So they mutually agreed between them to keep their encounter secret. That's the conversation I over-heard while in the church. Dr Blackwood said, "We don't want to give him every little piece of information from that evening, because he'll be distracted by it." That's because Dr Blackwood didn't want to have to explain to you, Detective, what he was doing there. And Mr Harris agreed because he didn't want anyone to know he'd been there. He'd even asked his wife to provide a false alibi.'

'What do you make of this, Mr Harris?' asked the detective.

'Doesn't make any sense to me.'

'I'm struggling to understand, too,' said the detective.

'Mr Harris pretended he hadn't seen Dr Blackwood, and Dr Blackwood pretended he hadn't seen Mr Harris,' said

Lottie. 'The agreement benefitted them both. But as time passed, I think Mr Harris grew worried about Dr Blackwood keeping his word. Once Miss Trent had confirmed Dr Blackwood was her alibi for that evening, everyone knew Dr Blackwood had been in the grounds of the house. The police were likely to ask him more questions about what he saw while he was there. Mr Harris probably feared Dr Blackwood would tell the police he saw him heading towards the boathouse shortly before Lady Florence was murdered.'

'Are you suggesting Mr Harris murdered Dr Blackwood to silence him?' asked the detective.

'Yes,' said Lottie. 'He didn't want Dr Blackwood to tell anyone he'd seen him near the boathouse that evening. So he decided to push him off the cliff and hoped it would look like he'd accidentally fallen.'

'Luckily, we had that witness in the boat who saw it,' said Detective Lynton. 'But there's still something missing, Miss Sprigg. Why would Mr Harris want to murder Lady Florence?'

Chapter Fifty-Nine

'AND THAT's what I want to know too,' said Miss Trent. 'Arthur served Lady Florence loyally for decades!'

'Yes, he did,' said Lottie. 'But then he was very disappointed when that loyalty wasn't returned.'

'You'll need to explain this a bit better,' said Detective Lynton.

'Everyone is familiar with the sad story of Arthur's son, Tom,' said Lottie.

'Leave him out of it!' growled Mr Harris.

'Let's allow Miss Sprigg to continue,' said the detective.

'Tom Harris was working as a waiter at the seafood restaurant in the harbour,' said Lottie. 'But he lost his job when a customer complained about him. That customer was Lady Florence.'

'How do you know that?' said Miss Trent.

'I visited the seafood restaurant yesterday lunchtime,' said Lottie. 'Lady Florence was known for her grumpiness and the thought crossed my mind that she could have been the customer who'd complained about Tom Harris. I spoke to a waitress there who told me all about it.'

Detective Lynton turned to Arthur Harris. 'Did you know Lady Florence complained about your son?'

The man shrugged and said nothing.

Lottie continued, 'Tom Harris couldn't find work anywhere else. He couldn't provide for his wife and two children. And then he began to drink too much. Most of the pubs in Fernwood-on-Sea won't let him in now. That's what the waitress told me. Tom Harris's wife left him and moved in with Mr Harris and his wife with her two children. I imagine it must be quite crowded in their small cottage. Presumably Mr Harris has been doing all he can to support his family. I think he might have been desperate enough to appeal to Lady Florence for help.'

'Did you?' the detective asked him.

Mr Harris shrugged again. 'Lady Florence was aware of my circumstances and what had caused them.'

'Would you care to explain some more?'

'Let's hear how Miss Sprigg explains it first.'

'I can only guess Mr Harris must have asked Lady Florence for help. After all, she helped Miss Trent's mother when her home was almost bought by Mrs Fitzroy.'

'And I wasn't going to put the rent up,' said Mrs Fitzroy. 'That was just Lady Florence's scaremongering.'

'So you think Mr Harris asked Lady Florence for help, Miss Sprigg?' asked Detective Lynton.

'He might have done. Perhaps he asked for a loan or an increase in his wages. I suspect Lady Florence refused.'

'Did she?' the detective asked Mr Harris.

He folded his arms and said nothing.

'Perhaps Mr Harris tried again to ask for Lady Florence's help on the night of her death,' said Lottie. 'He would have seen Captain O'Malley's boat on the beach and would have waited for him to leave the boathouse and row away.

'Mr Harris must have been angry at Lady Florence for

causing his son to lose his livelihood and turn to drink. And he must have grown even angrier when she refused to help him and his family. In a fit of anger, I think he grabbed the wrench which was stored on the boathouse wall and he struck her with it.'

'No,' said Miss Trent.

'Is this true?' Detective Lynton asked Mr Harris. 'Did you have a conversation with Lady Florence in the boat shed?'

Mr Harris took off his cap and scratched his bald head. 'People said I was foolish for being loyal to Lady Florence,' he said. 'I really thought she would help me and my family in a time of need. I know Tom may have not been the best waiter, but he tried his hardest. She told the manager of the restaurant she wouldn't go there again if Tom still worked there. Word got round he was unreliable and he couldn't find any other work.

'When I explained to her I was having to support Tom's family, she refused to listen. I'd worked for a pittance for a long time and I hadn't minded so much when I was only supporting my wife. But with three extra mouths to feed, the money didn't go far enough. The wage I asked for was the same as I'd have got anywhere else. But she refused. I suppose I could have got a job elsewhere. But then I'd have had to have moved out of the cottage on her land. And besides, I was angry.

'Like Captain O'Malley, I lost my temper with her that evening. However, he walked away before he did something he regretted.' He gave a sniff. 'I didn't manage to do the same.'

There was a long pause.

'You asked your wife to provide a false alibi?' asked the detective.

'Yes. I think she knew what I'd done that evening. But she was angry with Lady Florence too. So she lied to protect me and our family.'

'And Dr Blackwood?' asked the detective.

'I didn't trust him. I knew that he knew I did it. It was only going to be a matter of time until he told someone he saw me there. Perhaps he planned to blackmail me? I certainly had no money to pay him off. Once his secret about Miss Trent was out, he had no need to keep my secret anymore. So I gave him a shove when we were walking on the cliff top. I hoped everyone would think it was an accident. I didn't spot the boat out there with the person who saw it.'

'I'm sorry I dropped you in it, Arthur,' said Captain O'Malley. 'I didn't know it was you on the clifftop. I just saw the man get pushed, and I had to tell Detective Lynton what I saw. I couldn't let it pass.'

'No, I suppose not. But you've admitted to being a smuggler, Captain O'Malley, so that makes two of us in trouble today.'

Detective Lynton nodded to the sergeant, and the two men were put in handcuffs.

Chapter Sixty

'I STILL CAN'T BELIEVE Arthur Harris is a murderer,' said Miss Trent. Lottie and Mrs Moore sat with her on the terrace of Tidecrest House. The sun was setting over the headland of Windy Edge and the sky was turning a beautiful shade of orange. Duke trotted around the garden with a ball in his mouth and Rosie followed him, hoping he might drop it for her.

'He doesn't seem the type, does he?' said Mrs Moore. 'How wrong I was about the murders being connected to the smuggling operation!'

'You weren't completely wrong,' said Lottie. 'You reported it to Detective Lynton, and the police found the contraband in the cave.'

'That's true.'

'And I'm annoyed that the village gossip, Mrs Collins, was right about the illegitimate child,' said Miss Trent. 'I refused to believe it! I really thought Lady Florence would have told me about it. And I almost feel a little bit sorry for Victoria Fitzroy. She never had a happy relationship with her mother.

As much as I like to grumble about my mother, I've learned now to feel a little more grateful for her.'

'That's the spirit, Miss Trent,' said Mrs Moore. 'It's a sorry tale, but perhaps there's something which the rest of us can learn from.'

'I shall help Arthur Harris's family and make sure they're provided for,' said Miss Trent. 'And hopefully young Tom Harris will be able to mend his ways before long.'

'He could probably do with a second chance,' said Mrs Moore. 'If he promises to cut down on his drinking, perhaps there's a job on the estate he could do?'

'His father's job,' said Miss Trent. 'I'm going to be a bit lost without Arthur now the police have hauled him away.'

'Well, I'd like to thank you, Marianne, for having Lottie and me to stay while you went through a most horrid time.'

'No, my thanks must go to you, Mrs Moore. I'd have been lost without the pair of you being here.'

'I'm sorry we suspected you.'

'Oh, that's because I was being secretive. I brought it on myself. Everything was sorted in the end.'

'If it's alright with you, we'll head back to London tomorrow and leave you in peace.'

'Oh, must you? Please stay until the weekend.'

'Are you sure?'

'Yes. It will be nice to have a few days together when we're not all talking about murder.'

'Since you put it like that, it would, Marianne. And we've been beside the sea all this time and I haven't even had a swim yet.'

'Let's do it tomorrow. The forecast looks good.'

'Do you fancy a bathe tomorrow, Lottie?'

'Yes, I do. The only other thing I need to do tomorrow is post a letter.'

'To whom?'

'Josephine Holmes. I still haven't written my reply to her, so I need to go and do it now.'

THE END

* * *

Thank you

Thank you for reading this Lottie Sprigg mystery. I really hope you enjoyed it! Here are a few ways to stay in touch:

- Join my mailing list and receive a FREE short story *Murder at the Castle*: marthabond.com/murder-at-the-castle
- Like my brand new Facebook page: facebook.com/marthabondauthor

A free Lottie Sprigg mystery

Find out what happens when Lottie, Rosie and Mrs Moore visit Scotland in this free mystery *Murder at the Castle*!

When Lottie Sprigg accompanies her employer to New Year celebrations in a Scottish castle, she's excited about her first ever Hogmanay. The guests are in party spirits and enjoying the pipe band, dancing and whisky.

But the mood turns when a guest is found dead in the billiard room. Who committed the crime? With the local police stuck in the snow, Lottie puts her sleuthing skills to the test. She makes good progress until someone takes drastic action to stop her uncovering the truth...

Visit my website to claim your free copy:
marthabond.com/murder-at-the-castle

Or scan the code on the following page:

Also by Martha Bond

Lottie Sprigg Country House Mystery Series:

Murder in the Library
Murder in the Grotto
Murder in the Maze
Murder in the Bay

Lottie Sprigg Travels Mystery Series:

Murder in Venice
Murder in Paris
Murder in Cairo
Murder in Monaco
Murder in Vienna

Writing as Emily Organ:

Augusta Peel Mystery Series:

Death in Soho

ALSO BY MARTHA BOND

Murder in the Air
The Bloomsbury Murder
The Tower Bridge Murder
Death in Westminster
Murder on the Thames
The Baker Street Murders
Death in Kensington

Penny Green Mystery Series:

Limelight
The Rookery
The Maid's Secret
The Inventor
Curse of the Poppy
The Bermondsey Poisoner
An Unwelcome Guest
Death at the Workhouse
The Gang of St Bride's
Murder in Ratcliffe
The Egyptian Mystery
The Camden Spiritualist

Churchill & Pemberley Mystery Series:

Tragedy at Piddleton Hotel
Murder in Cold Mud
Puzzle in Poppleford Wood
Trouble in the Churchyard
Wheels of Peril
The Poisoned Peer
Fiasco at the Jam Factory
Disaster at the Christmas Dinner
Christmas Calamity at the Vicarage (novella)